For Christine and Mike
with many abrazos,

Carter

MAYA
GODS & MONSTERS

MAYA
GODS & MONSTERS

STORIES
by CAROL KARASIK

ILLUSTRATIONS
by ALFONSO HUERTA

SUPERNATURAL STORIES FROM THE UNDERWORLD AND BEYOND

THRUMS
BOOKS

OTHER BOOKS by Carol Karasik

Maya Threads: A Woven History of Chiapas,
with Walter F. Morris, Jr.

The Drum Wars: A Modern Maya Story

The Turquoise Trail:
Culture and Jewelry of the American Southwest

EDITOR/PUBLISHER: Linda Ligon
ASSOCIATE PUBLISHER: Karen Brock
DESIGNER: Susan Wasinger
TEXT: ©2016 Carol Karasik
ILLUSTRATIONS: © 2016 Alfonso Huerta except where noted

Library of Congress Control Number: 2016954660

THRUMS
BOOKS

Thrums Books
306 North Washington Avenue
Loveland, Colorado 80537 U.S.A.

Printed in China through Asia Pacific Offset

For XUN and MAXAM

TABLE OF CONTENTS

Maya Gods and Monsters

The MAYA GODS

All these stories have many versions.
All these gods have many faces.

Maya gods and goddesses live in a private world.

They seldom interfere in the great and small affairs of humanity.

They created human beings who would praise them, that is all.

When they are not summoned through offerings and prayers, they keep to themselves.

Left on their own, they change places, they multiply,

split in two, four, six, eight, and so on.

Perhaps they are part of one divine being, who is already two—Our Mother-Father.

It's no wonder that they created the world many times.

This, the fourth creation, began when the gods set up three stones in the center

of the universe. The stones are three stars in the constellation Orion.

The stones formed the first hearth, which the gods circle,

just as families sit around the fire in the middle of their houses,

eating, talking, and telling stories.

The gods are like a large family, made up of different personalities

and different powers,

but each depends on the other for their existence.

We praise their great and generous spirits for this life.

The
THREE CREATIONS
A MULTITUDE of BLUNDERS

ong before people inhabited the earth, the gods filled the world with noise. They hadn't planned it that way, but all the amazing creatures they made—jaguars, howler monkeys, rattlesnakes, black-winged chachalacas—cackled and roared and hissed incessantly.

"*Witz, witz, witz,*" said the rat. "*Xpurpuwek, xpurpuwek,*" cried Whippoorwill. The gods couldn't sleep or think.

"They know how to grunt and squawk, but they don't know how to pray. They can't even pronounce our names. And those rabbits and hairless dogs are always gossiping and telling tall tales. Soon they'll be stealing our secrets," the Creators complained.

"All right, then. We'll just let them slink around the Underworld, steal through the forests, beat their wings against the sky until they are hunted down and eaten." And so the gods decreed that the animals, birds, and insects would become food for one another.

The next race of beings didn't talk at all because the gods made them out of mud. Those people just waddled about aimlessly. They had

no backbones, they had no brains. They were just crumbling lumps with lopsided faces. The mud people simply melted away in the rain.

The gods hung their heads in disappointment. "We've made a terrible mistake," they said. "But let's try again. Let's make people who know how to praise us."

Next the gods made people out of wood, but the people of wood had no hearts or minds or blood or fat. They were as stiff as sticks, dry as bricks, and when they spoke, they had nothing good to say. And so the gods decided to destroy those stubborn, heartless, witless creatures.

Monsters with needle teeth chewed their wooden arms and crunched their legs.

Their dogs snapped and snarled. "You cold-blooded people never fed us properly. Now we'll take a bite out of your stubborn shins."

The grinding stones crushed their ribs. "All you've done is cause us pain. Screech, scratch, *huqui, huqui!* Now we'll do the same to you."

The cooking pots rose up in anger. "You burned our bottoms. Our mouths are black," screaked the pots. "Now we'll toss you into the fire."

The Lord of Thunderbolts sent down a rain of black pitch that darkened the earth and drowned the wooden people for good. Those that escaped to the trees turned into monkeys.

The flood washed away everything on earth. The sky collapsed and the mountains sank. There was no earth and there was no sky. All that was left was an ocean of water, and a deep, dark silence.

ITZAMNA

and the

FOURTH WORLD

The Endless Creation

ITZAMNA
and the
FOURTH WORLD

 ld Itzamna, the highest of the gods, was floating on his back in the middle of the sea, just daydreaming about this and that, when a brilliant idea popped into his head. He clapped his hands, and the seven Gods of Creation, who were quietly snoozing on their reed mats, sat bolt upright.

"You know," said Itzamna, "we should really make a new world. We need more excitement. We need some better company."

"It's true," the gods agreed. "But we've had bad luck before, and now look at the state we're in."

"I'm just circling around without rhyme or reason," moaned the old Sun, Lord of Time.

"I'm so waterlogged I'm beginning to lose my powers," the Lord of Thunder sputtered.

"Yes, I can't remember who I am," sighed the Lord of Death.

"Just as well," said the others.

Itzamna peered into his magic mirror and saw the world as it was and would be. He saw the reflections of the gods, who were reflections of

himself, multiplying endlessly. The image of the world was also multiplying—world after world after world, doubling, tripling, and quadrupling until they were bubbling over the edge of his black mirror.

"We need order!" cried Itzamna, and without wasting another word, he started giving the Creator Gods instructions.

First they unraveled their silken cords and measured out the universe. They stretched the cords and laid out the four directions, east, west, north, and south. They created a perfect square. If you could look down upon it from a spot beyond infinity—which is impossible because infinity is too vast to see or imagine—the square would resemble a four-petaled flower.

"Excellent!" said Itzamna. The fallen sky was still lying upon the water, and there was hardly any room to walk around and breathe. "But we'll need more space for our new world. And we'll need a place to build a fire."

Just then, two gods came paddling along in their dugout canoe.

"Blood?" said one.

"Liar?" said the other.

"Wrong!" said Itzamna. "I said world. I said fire!"

"Wormbird, sire?" said the bowman, straightening his bashed-in jaguar helmet. "That sounds positively delicious! In which case, we'll be staying for supper."

"But where will we fry her?" asked the other paddler, twisting the dreadful stingray spine he wore through his nose. The two of them were as deaf as moles and as contrary as day and night.

"We've been paddling around this whirlpool forever and a week," muttered the Jaguar Paddler.

"That's if you call a fever a leak," the Stingray Paddler said with a sneer.

"There's no one living or dead to ferry, and besides…"

ITZAMNA
and the
FOURTH
WORLD

"It's darker than a vat full of chocolates."

"I've never seen a bat full of pockets, have you?"

"I've never seen an iguana wrap his tail around his ears," said the Stingray Paddler, pointing his bony finger at Itzamna who was turning into a storm, a stork, a lizard with blue feathers.

In the center of the four-petaled flower, where the oceanic sky and celestial sea came together, the three old gods placed three round stones. The three stones formed the hearth where the fire of creation would blaze forth.

Now Thunderbolt and the Plumed Serpent were in the middle of the waters, stirring the waves with their thoughts and worries. "How shall we make the earth?" they asked themselves and each other. "How shall we bring the world to life?"

Itzamna's melodious voice floated across the waters. As if by magic, his words became the things he uttered.

"Earth," he said, and the earth lifted her huge body from the deep.

"Stone," and mountains of jade and turquoise rose from the green plains.

"Light," and little flames flickered in the eyes and hearts of trees, bees, flowers, fleas, fish, deer, and opossums.

With each word, a new marvel sprang to life. Thrush. Crystal. Tapir. Banana. And as his words echoed throughout the world, Itzamna instantly invented writing and wrote the words down on paper.

Now some will tell you that the Plumed Serpent spoke the words. Others will tell you that it was Thunderbolt. Some will even tell you that the creation of the earth happened in an entirely different way, not through words but a terrible tug of war.

You see, Itzamna was a great sorcerer and shape-shifter. Disguised as the god of night, Tezcatlipoca, he went off to rouse the Earth Monster, who was lurking at the bottom of the primordial sea. This monster looked like a cross between a crocodile and a slimy blood-sucking toad.

Tezcatlipoca called to her, "Hoooooo," but nothing stirred, not even a ripple.

Then he stuck out his big toe to lure her from the muck. Before he could wiggle his big toe twice, she swallowed his foot in one gulp. Ooooh, his screams were louder than the waves slapping against the monster's hideous teeth and claws.

Hearing Tezcatlipoca's cries, the Plumed Serpent rushed in to help. Immediately he grabbed the monster by the right arm and left leg and coiled himself around her. Tezcatlipoca grabbed the left arm and right leg. The two gods twisted and pulled until, with one big bone-splitting crack, they ripped the monster in two. Then they heaved her, warts and all, out of the turbulent waters. One half of her went to

dwell in the sky. The other half became the earth. The beast's bumps and ridges grew into mountains. Trees and flowers sprouted from her hair, springs and rivers poured from her weeping eyes.

While she was thrashing about and wailing, Tezcatlipoca's wounded foot turned into a black obsidian mirror wreathed in curls of smoke. When he walked he made no sound. The monster couldn't hear him limping across the bridge of her nose or climbing up and down the steep mountains of her back. When he reached the place where the three hearthstones lay, the Lord of Night stood very still. Then he spun on his mirrored heel and created fire.

Tezcatlipoca kept on spinning, and as he spun he turned into a mirrored tree whose spreading branches, spiraling upward, lifted the monstrous sky high above the earth. Round and round he whirled, filling the sky with stars. All the stars began whirling, and the great wheel of time started turning with the same steady motion as the stars.

The tree turned into an iguana, the iguana turned into Itzamna, and as soon as he was himself again he split himself in four. Each of his four selves raised its iguana tail and lifted up the four corners of the earth. That's why Earth is called "Iguana House."

But Itzamna is always changing.

Sometimes he takes the shape of a serpent and sprouts wings. "*Woo-koo, woo-koo!*" he cries.

Sometimes he becomes the giant crocodile that carries the earth on its back. All day he lazes by the river, watching butterflies land on his snout. He is so quiet and still that trees take root and grow from his wrinkled hide. When darkness falls, he wades across the hollows of the sky and becomes the starry path of the Milky Way. His belly is the center of our galaxy.

The old iguana is a supreme wizard and magician. Draped in darkness, he moves among the great and small, stitching the leaves, mending the stars, healing the birds. He is the wind whispering in the ear of the sleeping Sun, the celestial vapor embracing the Moon. Itzamna is everything he made and watches over.

He lives in water,

shapes the rain,

lights the fire,

plows the dirt,

comes from the iron bell of the earth,

and his heart rings.

Skin made of moss,

beard made of catfish whiskers,

head sprouting antlers,

hair hiding birds.

Ants and lightning live inside him.

His arms are wings.

"Sunlight," he whispers when he sways

over the branches of the Milky Way.

The DAWNING OF THE SUN and MOON

Before the sun had risen and people came to dwell on the surface of the earth, Itzamna was an entirely different sort of bird. He used to be a giant macaw whose silver eyes and jeweled teeth dazzled like the sun.

When he wasn't catching snakes, the proud and boastful Seven Macaw would fly about screeching, "Look at me! I am the sun, I am the moon." All those who were waiting in the dim light for the coming of the first dawn got tired of it. "If only someone would get rid of that noisy parrot," they grumbled.

As soon as the twin boys Hunahpu and Xbalanque heard about it, they grabbed their blowguns and began hunting the fabulous bird. Crouched in the bushes, they watched him as he dove out of the sky and perched in his favorite fruit tree. And while he was preening his scarlet feathers, the boys shot him with their blowguns and hit him squarely in the jaw.

The wounded bird landed with a crash. His dazzling teeth were rattling, his crumpled metal eyes were bulging in his aching head. "Ouch!" he screeched. Now he looked like a turkey vulture.

A little while later, two curers happened along, carrying a bag full of dental equipment. "We'll fix you up!" they said and quickly yanked out all his precious teeth. They left that vain macaw ragged and dejected, an empty shadow of bedraggled feathers. Now he circles the night sky as the star bird some call the Big Dipper.

The heroic twins lived with their grandmother, Xmucane, who gave them no love or affection. She ignored them when they cried and certainly never fed them. The boys had to do everything for themselves. Now their father had two older sons who were left behind in Xmucane's not-so-tender care. The older brothers were great artists and musicians who loved to entertain their grandmother. They were also good at dreaming up vicious pranks to play on their little brothers, like sitting them on an anthill and stealing all their food. Xmucane always took their side.

"I'm sick of their tricks," said Hunahpu to Xbalanque as they were walking through the forest. "They'd be happy to let us starve."

"They paint and write very well," said Xbalanque to Hunahpu, "but they behave like wild monkeys."

Just then the boys discovered a tree full of luscious fruits, and they started jumping and whooping for joy. "Let's run home right away and tell our older brothers. These fruits were meant for them."

The older brothers couldn't wait to climb the tree, but as they climbed, the tree grew higher and higher until it almost touched the sky.

"Help!" they hollered.

"Turn your loincloths around so the flap hangs in back. That should help," Hunahpu suggested.

The older brothers did as they were told, and the minute their loincloths were flapping like tails, Hunahpu and Xbalanque turned them into monkeys. The boys laughed themselves silly, but oh, their grandmother cried and cried.

The old woman had never told the boys how their father and his twin brother had disappeared. Yes, her own dear sons, One Hunahpu and Seven Hunahpu, went off to the caves beneath the earth and never came back, and the old woman never stopped weeping and waiting for their return. "My sons are lost forever in the Underworld of Xibalba," she sobbed to herself, and the light in her heart grew fainter. Yes, it was a very sad story, but the boys had to find out for themselves.

When One Hunahpu and Seven Hunahpu were still living on the surface of the earth, they did nothing but play ball, and the racket really upset the lords living down in the Underworld.

"Who's that kicking and bouncing over our heads? It sounds like a pack of wild boar," they grumbled.

"Let's teach them some respect," said Pus Master and Jaundice Master. "We'll make them swell up and turn yellow."

"I'll grind them down to skin and bones," said Skull Scepter.

"I'll puncture them in the belly," said Stab Master.

"And I'll catch the blood," said Blood Gatherer.

"Then they'll die for sure," said One Death and Seven Death.

The gods were really in a huff. So they sent four messengers to invite the brothers down to play a game with the Lords of Death. The owl messengers had sharp wings but no legs, beaks like daggers,

and one owl had no head at all. The brothers could hardly refuse.

They followed the owls down a steep canyon, crossed the river of spikes, crossed the river of blood, and stumbled down the black road to Xibalba. By the time they arrived, all the lords were laughing so hard their bones were rattling. "You're already finished," they said. The brothers didn't even have a chance to play the ball game. The Lords of Death sacrificed them, buried them, and hung the head of One Hunahpu in a cacao tree that was growing beside the ball court. As soon as they placed the head in the fork of the tree, the tree bore delicious chocolate fruits. All of Xibalba was forbidden to go near it.

One day a beautiful girl came along. Her name was Blood Woman, and she was the daughter of Blood Gatherer. As she was reaching up to pluck the sweet fruits from the tree, the head of One Hunahpu spoke to her.

"Why would you want the bones from this tree?" said the head of One Hunahpu.

"You think they're tasty, you think they're sweet, these hard black seeds in a white shell?"

"I do," said Blood Woman.

"Well, I will give you a sign for my firstborn sons.

Tell them their father hasn't disappeared. He is alive and will go on living." And the skull spit in the girl's hand. Immediately she conceived.

Pretty soon her horrible father noticed she had something growing in her belly, and his hollow eyes burned red with rage. "Bring me her heart!" he commanded.

Blood Woman escaped through a hole in the earth and fled to the house of One Hunahpu's mother. It wasn't easy putting up with Xmucane's miserable temper. The suspicious old crone didn't want that girl around and said so whenever she had the chance. Still, her stubbornness was no match for Blood Woman's brains and magic powers, which she naturally passed on to her beautiful twin boys, Hunahpu and Xbalanque.

"Cry babies," Xmucane called them the moment they were born. And so they went to live in the mountains, and when they grew up they became great hunters

"Why would you want the bones from this tree?" said the head of One Hunahpu.

and ballplayers. The clever boys learned everything on their own.

Every gray, sunless day the boys practiced ball, and every gray, sunless day the Lords of Death woke up fuming and cursing. They couldn't help it. The sound of the bouncing rubber ball was giving them a splitting headache. "Who's that kicking and banging over our heads?" they grumbled. "What nerve!"

Again they sent their owl messengers to the surface of the earth. But the boys were playing in the ball court and only their grandmother was at home to receive the bad news.

Old Xmucane gave the message to a tiny louse, but on the way, the louse was swallowed by a toad, the toad was swallowed by a snake, and the snake was swallowed by a laughing falcon. When the falcon reached the ball court, he called out, "Woo-koo! I have a message in my belly."

The falcon spit out the snake, the snake spit out the toad, and the toad spit out the louse, who said, "In seven days you are to come and play ball with the Lords of Death."

Down they went to the Underworld, down the steep canyon, across Pus River and across Blood River, and when they arrived they greeted the Lords of Xibalba most cordially, because a mosquito had already whispered their secret names:

"Good morning, One Death, Seven Death, House Corner, Blood Gatherer.

"Good morning, Pus Master, Jaundice Master, Bone Scepter, Skull Scepter.

"Good morning, Wing, Packstrap, Bloody Teeth, Bloody Claws."

The Lords of Xibalba weren't laughing now.

Every day the twins played ball against the Lords of Death. And every day the twins outsmarted them. Every night the Lords of Xibalba put them through a dangerous test, and every night the twins tricked them.

First the lords locked the boys in Dark House and gave them a torch and a lit cigar. "Don't let the flame die," they were told. The boys put red macaw feathers at the end of the torch and a glowing firefly on the tip of the big cigar, and in the morning, the torch and cigar were as good as new.

They locked the boys in Razor House, but the knives that were supposed to slice them in two refused to move and stuck their razor-sharp points in the ground.

They locked the boys in Cold House, but the boys drove out the ice and wind and hail.

The lords locked the boys in Jaguar House, but Hunahpu and Xbalanque fed the jaguars animal bones, and the jaguars didn't eat them.

Next, they locked the boys in the House of Fire, but the boys were just lightly seared. The lords were amazed.

When the boys entered Bat House, they encountered monstrous snatch-bats, which had knives instead of noses. The boys just curled up inside their blowguns and went to sleep. But when Hunahpu stuck his head out to see what time it was, a bat snatched his head right off.

At that moment a coati came along, rolling a big squash. Xbalanque picked it up and carved a new head that looked and talked exactly like his handsome brother.

When the boys entered Bat House,

they encountered monstrous snatch-bats,

which had knives instead of noses.

The DAWNING OF THE SUN and MOON

The next morning, there were the lords, playing ball with Hunahpu's real head, bouncing and kicking it around the court. But Xbalanque intercepted and sent it flying into the woods. The Lords of Death went running after it, and in the excitement, Rabbit rescued the real head and gave it back to Hunahpu. The lords were no match for the boys and their animal helpers.

Even though the twins passed many tests and trials, the lords still hungered for their deaths. "We'll throw them into a burning oven," they howled. "That will put an end to them for sure."

But Hunahpu and Xbalanque heard their gleeful shrieking and came up with a clever plan. Willingly they sacrificed themselves and jumped into the raging fire. Their bones were ground as fine as flour and scattered in the river. Five days later, the boys reappeared as catfish, and the next day they appeared as poor vagabonds dressed in rags.

Disguised as wandering actors, they went to the palace and entertained the Lords of Death. They danced on stilts and performed many magic tricks. They sacrificed a dog and then revived it. They burned down a house full of demons and then raised it—walls, roof, devils, and all. The lords were filled with wonder and delight.

"Sacrifice yourselves!" they shrieked. "Let's see it now!"

Hunahpu sacrificed his brother and brought him back to life.

"Oh, this is wonderful!" cried One Death and Seven Death. They were crazy with joy. "Now do it to us! Sacrifice us!"

But the Lords of Xibalba did not come back to life. All the wicked creatures fled to the caves and canyons, shaking with fear. Ever since, death remains in the black shadows of the Underworld, feeding on sap and broken gourds and tormenting the guilty and wretched.

After their great triumph, the Hero Twins found their father and uncle and brought them back to life. Their father became the god of corn, who dies and is reborn each year.

Then the boys rose to heaven and became the sun and the moon.

The
GIFT OF CORN
BLOOD,
FLESH AND BONE

A tiny corn stalk sprouted from the body of One Hunahpu and started growing up through the long, dark passages of the Underworld. Finally it broke through a crack in the earth, put forth two huge ears of corn, and sank again into the soil. The seeds lay in heaps inside a secret cavern.

Coyote happened to be out scavenging in the mountains when he sniffed something sweet in the air. He followed the scent over the cliffs, and just as his mouth was beginning to water, he butted his nose against a great stone. No matter how hard he pawed and scraped, he couldn't find a way in. It seemed the scent was coming from a cave, and it was locked tight.

Coyote heard a woodpecker tap-ping at a tree. "Excuse me," he said, "there's something so much sweeter than mealy bugs inside this cave."

Woodpecker tapped at the rock until his beak was blunt, but he couldn't find the entrance either.

In a little while, an army of ants came parading along. "There's something sweet and wonderful in-side this cave," said Coyote. "You're little. Maybe you can find the door."

"No problem," said the ants, and

they filed right in and found heaps of yellow corn. "Mmm, this food is tastier than ginger petals," they cheeped. The captain, the sergeant, and every stouthearted soldier hoisted a kernel, and without wasting time, they marched straight to the palace of the gods.

"Mmm, this corn is ambrosial," said the gods. "It is the most marvelous food on earth. Bring us more!"

The ants skittered off, and a few days later, they delivered more corn for the gods. By now their backs were aching, their feet were sore, and they were huffing and puffing after their long march. The gods took pity on the little creatures. "We see you need some help," they said.

Chak, the rain god, flew to the mountain, and with one dazzling silver lightning bolt he split the sacred rock. There lay the golden treasure!

When the gods saw the mounds of gleaming kernels, they were overjoyed. "At last we've found the perfect substance to make a woman and a man. They will be full of strength and full of light."

The Creators carried the corn to the house of Xmucane, the grandmother of the Hero Twins. She ground it on her grinding stone until the corn meal was as fine as powder. Then she spit on it to add some grease, and the gods offered drops of their own blood to the mixture. And with this holy corn meal, they made the skin and bones of human beings.

They were beautiful in every way. The women tied their hair in tassels. Their arms fluttered like corn leaves in the wind. They used the kernels of their teeth to eat, and to measure cloth and string. These men and women were able to talk properly and to praise the gods with beautiful words. They knew how to walk, they knew how to think, and they knew how to work. When spring came, they planted the corn seeds in rows. When autumn came, they harvested their corn and had enough to eat all winter. They wouldn't have to search the woods for nuts or grubs or rely on wild greens and berries. They wouldn't have to eat stone soup. There would be enough corn to feed them and enough to sustain the gods.

And so the people multiplied and spread across the mountains and plains. They hoed and weeded, and when they weren't tilling the fields they built magnificent temples where they worshipped the god of corn. And when the cities fell, the people moved on. They knew in their hearts that everything—kingdoms, people, animals, plants, and stars—were part of the same natural cycle, growing, dying, and coming back to life.

~

But corn is hard work, and some people are lazy. Once there was a farmer who was out clearing his land, but after he cut down a few bushes he was already worn out.

The man said to himself, "When Hunahpu and Xbalanque were still ordinary boys and had to tend their grandmother's fields, their axes and hoes did all the work. The soil turned itself and the trees fell on their own. I wish my axe and hoe, my land and trees could do the same."

He was lying on his back, about to take a nap, when he noticed a buzzard circling in the sky. "Oh buzzard," he called. "You just fly around and find your food. You don't have to sweat and toil."

The buzzard swooped down and spoke to the man. "But first I have to see the fumes rising from the carcass. For that I have to fly around all day. It's harder than you think," said the buzzard. "Why, the way you were lying there, stretched out, I thought you were a corpse."

"Yes, just look at me, all bent over and full of blisters. I'm always fighting off ants and aphids. I have to compete with mice and deer."

"But corn can grow everywhere—mountains, swamps, and deserts," replied the buzzard.

"There's so much life swarming over and under my plants. It's really too much," the man whined. "And sooner or later, everything that grows in this forest will rot and die. The earth gives us sustenance and then she takes it away."

"But life comes from dead things," said the buzzard. "I ought to know."

"Well, if you don't mind it, why don't we change places?"

So the man put on the buzzard's wings and flew away. The buzzard put on the man's pants and started working. He cleared the man's field,

planted the man's corn seeds, and then went home to the man's wife.

"You stink like a buzzard!" she said.

"Oh, it's just because I've been working so hard," said the buzzard.

Every day he went out to weed the fields. Thanks to Our Holy Sun and Chak, the rain god, there was an abundance of corn in September. The buzzard harvested his corn and hauled it to the man's house. Stooped and bent under his heavy burden, occasionally stopping to wipe away the sweat, he plodded along, just as the gods carried the days on their backs over the hills toward home.

"All this hard labor is worth it," the buzzard thought. "It's easier than searching for my meals."

The man's wife was delighted. Up at the crack of dawn, she soaked the kernels, then knelt before her stone *metate* and ground the corn into meal. She was careful not to drop a single kernel, because corn has human feelings. It cries if it is dropped or stepped on.

The woman made a small tortilla, and in the center, she punched three holes—two holes for eyes and a bigger hole for a mouth. She fed it to her baby, saying, "Here, my little one, open your mouth like this round tortilla and speak to me."

She gave a tortilla to the family dog, saying, "Here, dog, take your tortilla, you will carry me across the river to the Land of the Dead someday."

And then she made tamales stuffed with turkey and beans and fed them to her "husband," saying, "Thank you."

After eating six tamales, he patted his bloated stomach and burped. "There's something I've been meaning to tell you," he said. "You see, I'm not a man at all. I'm a buzzard. That's why I stink so much."

The woman thought about it a minute and then shrugged her shoulders. "That husband of mine was a worthless loafer. We never had anything to eat. Now I have plenty of corn and beans. I have white corn, yellow corn, red corn, blue corn, and black corn. I never have to worry. So what if you're a buzzard," she said. "I'm content. It's a small price to pay for a handful of Our Lord's sunbeams."

Hun Hunahpu,
the god of corn,

lives inside each kernel of the
corn plant. Hun Hunahpu,
the first father, lives inside
the Maya people. His spirit
is the essence of life that
grows and dies and renews
itself each spring,
now and forever.

K'INICH AHAU
EYE *of* THE SUN

I t makes no sense, but the Sun is always grumpy. You'd think he'd have a pleasant disposition, but being sunny and radiant every day is hard work. Up before the break of dawn, with only the stars and the planet Venus to guide him, he begins

his long, steep climb to the pinnacle of the sky. At noon, when he stops to catch his breath, he really has no time to rest. Gazing down upon the earth, he surveys the lives of all his creatures. Then he pulls out his pen and his thick gold ledger and makes a note beside each name: who is thieving, lying, or sleeping late, who is working and praying and content with the little bit they have. He writes it all down in his ledger—

name, place, date, and hour. If the sin is grave, he will send sickness upon the wicked immediately. Or he will wait. At the end of the world, some souls will rise to heaven and others will stay in the stinking black Underworld forever. The Sun is the one who keeps track. That's why people today call him Saint Salvador, the Judge. Otherwise, they'd call him a spy. High jinks, crimes— he's seen it all.

When he's finished writing, the Sun continues down his daily path. Now he's strolling under his big straw hat, a fancy dude heading for lunch at three. Now he's so tired he has to hold on to the cords that hang down from the sky, just to keep from stumbling off the trail. At sunset he's ready to sink into the ocean, which is filled with his golden treasures. Hot and weary, he crawls into his cave. Maybe his wife, the ever-changing goddess of the moon, has fixed him something good for supper or at least prepared an ice-cold bath. He likes to soak in his big stone tub until the bathwater boils and the air is steaming hot. Sometimes his wife whacks him with a eucalyptus branch, which is good for his circulation. Some people say she does it just to get his attention. "All right, I'm leaving now. I'm going to make my rounds," she says. But by then he is usually snoring.

Long ago, he worked even harder. Some swear that when he was younger he was the spitting image of Hunahpu, full of vim and vigor. But at night he prowled like a jag-

uar under the bone trees of the Underworld. At dawn he turned into a scarlet macaw streaking across the morning sky, or a hummingbird darting from flower to flower.

Others believed he was a golden puma leaping from his cave on Trogon Mountain. His tail whipped the grass, his claws scratched burning lines across the palace floor. At noon the king could hear the sounds of war and wailing. The pillars began trembling. "The puma is searching for ghosts," people said. "He has come for our souls."

But where would we be without the Sun? How would we eat or see? He is the eye of heaven and the burning heart, the Lord of Time keeping the days, months, and years in motion. He is the god of Number Four, who presides over the summer and winter solstices, lord of the northern and southern light as they rise and set at the four corners of the sky. The Sun and Number Four look exactly alike. They have the same T-shaped teeth, the same mirrored brow, and the same squint in their square eyes.

The day moves on. But as the Sun limps across the plaza and through the empty market, he is the image of every aging wanderer slipping slowly toward the grave.

In the red setting sun, the old man turns into a monkey, and in his monkey body he will mark the hours of the night. That jaguar prowling below him, fishing in the pool, is his animal spirit too, walking slowly eastward toward the dawn.

Alone he makes his earthly rounds, alone he will rise tomorrow, our life, our god, our mirror.

GRANDMOTHER
MOON
WEAVES *the* WORLD

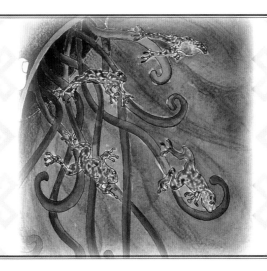

Long ago, when the world was new and time
was learning how to walk straight,
the crooked and crazy one who limped along,
or speeded up, or glided in perfect circles—

GRANDMOTHER
MOON

Our Grandmother Moon—floated like a beautiful girl into the arms of a ceiba tree.
  Her long lizard tail whipped the ground, her wild white hair curled
  around the branches.
  The pools of her eyes, the shadows of her fangs, shone brighter than day.
  The Mother of Waters swayed in the tree as if she were poling a long canoe
  across the night sea.

The ancestors thought she was fishing. They thought she was grinding corn.
  But her net was made from silken strands of her chin hair,
  her paddle was her weaving sword, and the grinding stone
  she was sweating over
  was a loom made of giant boughs.

"You pitiful, naked excuses!" said Grandmother Moon. "I'll show you how to make
  threads like mine to cover up those lazy bones."
  Round and round her spindle spun. All night the stars moved round,
  all night she wove and worked herself into a frenzy, and when morning came,
  her blouse was a world of flowers and toads.

All the earth's creatures are
woven together
in our clothes,
all rhythms,
all cycles,
all songs.
These the goddess
showed us.

LADY YELLOW RAMON LEAF

O nce the great sorcerer Itzamna fell in love with the young goddess of the moon. When he saw her gathering shafts of moonlight for her loom, he fell into a swoon and lost count of the stars and planets.

He followed her day and night, disguised as a blue iguana, disguised as a red-throated humming-bird. He watched her weave the south wind, he watched her when she went down to the river to bathe, disguised as the boulder she leaned on, disguised as the pebble under her left foot, disguised as the water rushing around her ankles. Instantly she felt an odd shiver and leapt onto the bank. He was the cattail reed she clung to, the leaves she used to dry her toes. She tried to escape, but he was everywhere, in the humid air, in the racket of the birds, in the oncoming night.

She tossed down her comb and ran. Her comb turned into brambles, but he changed into a quail and flew after.

She took off her jade earrings.

They turned into a cornfield, but he changed into a fox and chased her.

She sent a rabbit to distract him, but Itzamna wasn't fooled.

She threw down her necklace of pearls, which turned into the midnight mist, but he changed into the north wind and came after.

She dropped her silver sandals. They turned into shadows, but he became the Night Terror and pursued her past the dawn.

She unfastened her silver gown. It turned into a mirror, and he saw himself glowing like the rising sun. She disappeared in the light.

He turned into a cloud and caught her. The goddess gave him her love, because she loved everyone who loved her.

But she was as wayward as he, rising and setting in different places on the horizon, racing or rambling across the sky and always changing faces.

"Be still," he cried. "Be constant."

"I am the moon," she said with a bewitching smile.

Itzamna was exhausted by her fickleness. He was an old god after all, and even though he possessed all the magic in the world, he couldn't dream of enough ways to keep her. And so he turned the young moon into a ramon tree, older than creation.

Brown and motionless, she stood at the southern tip of paradise. Her roots reached deep into the Underworld and her branches brushed the sky. Her enormous leaves provided shade for the eter-

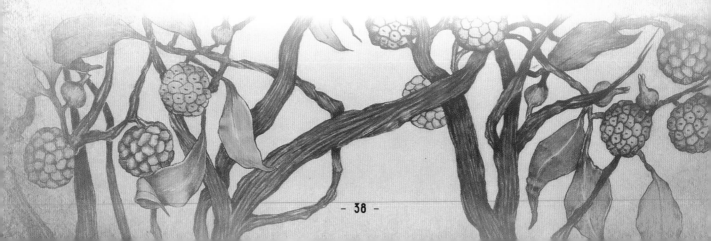

nal flowers. Her graceful limbs provided nuts for the animals, nesting places for the birds, and a soft bench for old Grandmother Moon when she paused on her nightly journey.

Eons passed without a rustle or a sigh. Lady Yellow Ramon Leaf became the mother tree of the forests and the mother tree of the gods. Out they stepped, one by one, whole and fully formed, from a cleft in her wide trunk. She cradled her divine children in her arms.

Itzamna was growing so absentminded he forgot about everything in the world. His heart turned to stone, his mind turned to sleep. Moths and butterflies lost their wings, the corn withered and died. Hunger tightened people's bellies, and they could barely pray.

Lady Yellow Ramon Leaf leaned down and spoke to them in a soothing voice. "Why bother shaking him?" she whispered. "He may wake up as thorny as the wilderness, as mean as a swamp. Even if he loves you, he may chase you until your feet turn to lead. It's better to leave him be."

Ever since, the wild nuts of the ramon tree provide food during times of famine. When the gods of wind and rain send plagues and torments, the goddess offers bread that tastes like chocolate. Those whose bones are twisted and feeble, those whose mouths are as dry as straw call her the moon tree, because inside every nutshell is a little moon that cures all sickness and heals all wounds.

CHAK
THE RAIN GOD

C hak, the rain god,
was sitting in his cave,
rumbling and grumbling.
Far off he heard a song
that rattled and rocked
like a summer storm:

Rain, rain,
it's falling again.
The fields are flooding,
the sun is black,
the wings of the corn
are yellow and damp.
Stop the lightning,
Stop the thunderclap!
Tin, tin, tin,
Pim, pom, pim!

"What kind of song is that?" he spouted. "Why, I'll just spatter them, drown them, strike them with lightning bolts and more floods." Oh, he was getting angrier by the minute.

"On second thought, maybe I *will* go away. Let them try to live without me!"

The rain slowed to a drizzle, then a drop. The land became so dry the palm trees curled and the brown earth cracked. It got so dusty under the hot sun that people's throats ached and their skin burned like fire. Then their minds started to sizzle, and they began to wonder if the rain would ever come again to soak their thirsty plants and provide enough water for cooking and bathing or just a little thimbleful to drink. It is then they offered prayers to Chak, the rain god.

Chak listened to the prayers with his big shell-shaped ears. He rubbed his long, runny nose and scratched his serpent scales. The mirrors on his skin flashed and his eyes rolled like ball lightning.

"Dragnats!" he fumed. "Platitudinous paupers!" Then he threw his axe, and thunder shook the whole earth.

"Let's see now," he roared. "Should I be good or should I be wilder? Should I sprinkle or should I pour? Should I dampen their souls or destroy them? Just which Chak shall I be?"

He thought and thought until his head ached and he began to twitch.

"Oh, enough of this insufferable pitter patter! I'm powerful enough to be all four!"

All at once he rushed from the four directions, east, west, north, and south. All four Chaks were carrying axes, spears, and darts as they whirled across the sky.

The Yellow Chak charged in from the south with blinding lightning storms.

The White Chak whipped out of the north on icy squalls that stung like frozen needles. The Black Chak came dancing with

- 41 -

the wicked west wind, holding his blazing torches aloft and brimming over with disease and death.

The Red Chak raced from the east, dumping buckets of bean rain and corn rain, though the crops weren't even in the ground yet.

Oh, the sky was torn every which way, churning and hissing like a barrelful of snakes.

"The weather's gone crazy again," farmers said. It was the worst record in history.

"Yes," Chak spat, "and it's only March. Just wait till June. I'll pepper them with purple hailstones. I'll do something even stranger." And he delivered a bath of black ashes followed by a rain of green frogs. "I'm un-pree-dict-able," he boomed, and broke into gales of laughter.

Frogs were croaking in the mountains, frogs were croaking by the sea. "Bah, they can call all they want. Sounds like a band of bass drums and a tuba to me. But before I bring on the deluge...."

Chak looked down upon the tattered world, and a tear came to his eye. He waved the lightning serpent in his right hand, and a luminous fog rolled across the face of the earth. "I've ruined everything," he groaned. Then he retreated glumly to his cave.

There he sat, melancholy and sad, in the darkest recesses. His slinky serpent daughters, who usually spent their days weaving in the grand salon, put away their looms and tried to console him. "Cheer up, papa," they said. "Take a rest," they said. But he paid no attention. All he did was sob.

At dawn they brought him a cup of sulfur tea, at noon, a plate of eels. At night they hauled out his treasure chest and lifted the creaky lid. The chest was overflowing with gold.

"Brackets! Brillfire!" he bawled.

"Oh, papa, you should be happy," his daughters told him. "After all, you own everything on earth—all the land, mountains, rivers, streams, jewels, silver, and gold."

"And you're so generous, papa. When you're in a good mood."

"Well, I'm not in a good mood now! I'm not sharing my land, my water, my emerald nuggets, or the slightest stroke of good luck. If anyone tries to build a house without asking my permission, I'll blow

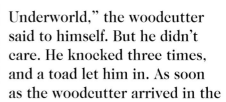

it away. They only love me for my money."

Chak's daughters could see he was in the midst of one of his famous fits, feeling sorry for the world and sorrier for himself, and they decided to let him sulk. "We're going out for a stroll now, papa. See you soon."

"Don't bring home any of those farmers!" Chak mumbled and went back to counting his coins. "Two trillion, ninety-six billion, fifty-five million, seven thousand, eight hundred and three. Two trillion, ninety-six billion, fifty-five million, seven thousand, eight hundred and four." He had a coin for every rainy day since the beginning of the first creation.

The moment they left the house, his serpent daughters changed into beautiful women wearing green silk ribbons in their long braids and fine brocaded blouses woven in a diamond design.

That day a young man who was out chopping wood caught sight of three mysterious maidens passing lightly along the trail. He was enchanted. Despite the heavy mist, he followed the daughters' delicate steps to the door of the cave.

"Oooh, this looks like the entrance to the Underworld," the woodcutter said to himself. But he didn't care. He knocked three times, and a toad let him in. As soon as the woodcutter arrived in the grand salon, the girls turned into horrible snakes. The cave filled with sulfurous smoke. Thunder roared, lightning crashed, sparks went flying in every direction. The woodcutter ran for his life!

"And don't come back!" Chak bellowed.

Then he turned to his three daughters. "Thanks, my girls. That's just what I needed. Now I'm feeling as right as rain."

It was the end of April, and Chak was in good spirits again. He mounted his white-tailed stag and went riding to Guatemala, to buy gunpowder for his lightning bolts.

While he was gone, his daughters stayed home, spinning cotton into clouds. The clouds piled up at the cave door, then rose and billowed in the sky. The frogs began their operatic croaking. Scorpion crawled out from under the rock where he was hiding and pricked the clouds with his long black tail.

Soon Chak will stomp and roar and lose his temper. Soon the water will fall like silver. Soon it will rain.

How the
GOD OF DEATH
LOST
HIS HAT

No one knows his name, but he is the great ruler of the Underworld. The other deadly lords wander in the darkness, bone-naked, without skin or hair, but not him. He often walks on the surface of the earth, and since he does, he can hardly go about his business looking like a skeletal rack of bones. No, he's a dignified old man, a little stooped and worn and skinny but nevertheless fit for polite human company.

You can tell he's a god and not an ordinary human being by the odd way he dresses. His cape is made of a jaguar skin, tail and all. The flaps of his loincloth are two rattlesnakes coiled at both ends. Instead of wearing sandals, he shuffles along in a pair of jaguar-paw slippers.

"Old Jaguar Foot" they call him when he's skulking beside the road in winter.

He skulks beside the road because he is also the patron god of merchants, especially merchants who travel the roads on winter nights. Most of them are chocolate sellers who need to deliver freshly picked cacao beans to their high-paying customers as fast as they can. They say they can make better time at

night getting from one place to another. What they don't say is that merchants are notorious spies, gossips, talebearers, and worse, and often have to leave town in a hurry. Of course, night is the time when demons wander, and traders who are lost or being chased know they can depend on Death for help. Old Jaguar Foot is a master of disguise in his old man's body. He knows the road and the right direction. Just follow the footprints painted on his loincloth and the spots on his jaguar tail!

And so he seldom sleeps. How could he? The hat he wears on his wrinkled head is a giant, black-winged screech owl. It's Old Jaguar Foot's pride and joy. Innumerable creatures would give everything they had to own that fabulous hat.

One night he was relaxing on his throne, smoking a cigar and drinking hot chocolate. As usual, Rabbit was seated on the floor, writing in his journal, but tonight there wasn't much to write about, and he was just sucking on his ink brush, bored to tears. Finally he looked up.

"P-p-perhaps, your m-m-majesty, your lordship," Rabbit stammered, "p-p-perhaps you would let me borrow your, uh, m-m-magnificent hat."

"What's in that chocolate you've been drinking? You must be mad or tipsy," Old Jaguar Foot roared.

"P-p-perhaps for one night only, your p-peripatetic eminence. Or just an hour, s-s-sire, say the hour between midnight and one, or the p-p-precious hour before the drowsy dawn picks up his broom and sweeps the path of the sun."

Old Jaguar Foot was amused by Rabbit's persistence. "All right," he whispered. "I'll let you try it on for one minute. But only if you tell me a story."

"Well, s-s-sir, how about that golden moment during the creation when you were seated in the Underworld and ordering all the gods around?"

"No, no," sighed Old Jaguar Foot. "It always makes me sad to remember my past glories."

"Then perhaps your highness would care to hear the story of how you and the other Lords of Xibalba got your heads cut off by the Hero Twins?"

"You insolent little creature!" snarled the Lord of Death. "Why not tell the story of how you tried to steal Deer's antlers and got your tail pulled off instead?"

That made Rabbit mad. He jumped up,

grabbed Death's hat, clothes, and walking staff, and ran away. You could hear the owl screeching all the way to the surface of the earth. Owl brought some corn seeds with him and appeared at the same time as the rains. Everyone on earth was happy.

But Old Jaguar Foot was stark naked! Shaking and shivering, he went off to complain to Lord Sun. He wandered up and down the cold, windy corridors of the Underworld until he heard the Sun snoring in his cave.

"Don't you know it's after midnight and I have so much work to do tomorrow? Perhaps you haven't noticed, but the days are getting longer."

"Yes, but I have no clothes. And Rabbit stole my hat!"

"You won't be needing them now. After all, it's springtime. Why not let that wily Rabbit have a turn. And let me get some sleep!"

Old Jaguar Foot waited and waited, and finally the days grew shorter and the nights longer. One crisp autumn day, Rabbit came scurrying back with the hat.

"It's about time!" said Old Jaguar Foot. "Do that again and I'll grab your ears and throw you as far as the moon!"

But the next spring, just when the days were getting longer, Rabbit stole the hat again! "One more time and I'll trade you in for an armadillo!" shouted Old Jaguar Foot and snuck off to borrow a loincloth.

The hat he wears on his
wrinkled head is a giant, black-winged
screech owl. It's Old Jaguar Foot's
pride and joy.
Innumerable creatures would give
everything they had to own
that fabulous hat.

Old Jaguar Foot got his hat back by the darkening days of fall. He breathed a sigh, and life returned to normal. The plants withered, the flowers were gone, and only chocolate merchants were out traveling. All the birds had flown away, except for the screech owl, who was busy delivering messages. "Come down and pay me a visit," said the message. But no one wants to visit the Lord of Death. All alone he sat on his throne, smoking his cigar and drinking hot chocolate.

"Tell me a story, Rabbit, to while away the time. Tell me a story about my adventures on the road."

"I can think of nothing d-duller," said Rabbit. "I m-m-mean greater, sire. Certainly your l-l-lordship has acquired immense wealth and accomplished many remarkable feats. Frankly, I have often wondered how you manage to walk so far with a s-s-snake hanging in front and in back of your knees."

"Every once in a while, you may recall, I send helpers to do my trading for me."

"Ah, yes," said Rabbit. "I remember when Chak, the rain god, paddled a bundle of goods in his canoe, in exchange for..."

"My great owl hat!"

"What I've been really wondering, your lordship, sir, is what you have in that b-b-bundle? Cigar ashes, papayas, a dead body?"

"Hah! You'll never guess, even if you guess from now until the end of time, which, as we know, has no end. Not like your miserable little tail!"

"Uh, right, s-s-sir. It must be something choice then."

"I am the lord of merchants and a goodwill ambassador, happy to fulfill the desires of gods and kings. Of course, there's always a price for my favors. But you know, even Death can be kind and friendly. Why, I once brought the Aztec emperor a bundle full of feathers. To rulers of the most powerful Maya cities, I gave my generous support. By way of thanks, the king of Palenque, K'an Bahlam, honored me with a handsome, full-length portrait. Very clever of him, Rabbit. If I hadn't liked that king, I would have done what spies and merchants often do—call in the enemy hordes! Yes, war is just an everyday part of my business. Do you remember those terrible battles with the king of Calakmul?"

Old Jaguar Foot knew the story so well he could tell it in his sleep. By then it was spring and Rabbit made off with the hat.

Back and forth goes the hat, like the changes in the seasons. Back and forth goes the year, from light to darkness. It's an endless game that Rabbit plays in honor of summer and winter.

PAWAHTUN

There's another old man, Old Man Mountain. He lived inside a mountain, which is how he got his name, and when he finally crept outside toward the tail end of creation, no one took much notice. There were people living on the surface of the earth, demons lurking in the Underworld, and the sun, moon, and stars circling the sky. The Creators breathed a sigh of relief and held a large celebration. All the gods were fairly content with how things turned out and were happily congratulating one another, all except Chak, the rain god, who put a damper on the banquet.

"The sky," he roared. "It's always moving whenever I walk about."

"Perhaps you've had too much honey wine," said Itzamna. "The sky is perfectly still. It's everything inside it—clouds, birds, stars—that are moving."

"Now that I think of it, I've noticed a slight swing to the west," said the Sun.

"Hah! That's me whipping my

tail," said Grandmother Moon.

"You won't be laughing when the sky falls," spluttered Chak. "You'll be dangling in an immense nothingness. We have to put a stop to this irritating quiver."

The Creators wrinkled their weighty brows and gazed upon the strange dip in the heavens.

"The stars of heaven sting," moaned a distant voice. "Rain ruins my eyes when my belly rolls too low." It was the deep, mournful drone of the long-suffering Earth Monster.

"Would another mountain help?" suggested Thunderbolt. "Or giant stones?"

"Can't hold up the sky with fountains. Can't hold up the sky with groans," the Paddler Gods chimed in.

They had already eaten all the turkeys on the table and were about to paddle off when Old Jaguar Foot said, "I'll contribute a million chocolate trees to support the state of the world."

"A delicious digression," said Itzamna, stifling a yawn. The yawn became a bubble, the bubble turned into a fish, and the fish spawned a practical idea. "How about one of us?" he said, pointing to a quiet little god sitting alone in the corner.

You'd think the Lords of Creation would have picked a young man for the job, someone buff who looked like he'd been lifting weights. Instead, they chose an old decrepit god who was practically immobile.

"He may be a little unsteady on his feet, and he's already bent over. But compared to the rest of us, that old fellow has plenty of time on his hands. All he has to do is stand in one spot and keep the days and nights in order."

And so the gods placed the vast heavens upon Pawahtun's frail shoulders. "The sky might shudder from time to time, but it will never fall," they said. "The old man is a little mad, but he's as dependable as a boulder."

They didn't seem too concerned about Pawahtun's curious habits. He likes to whistle through his two good teeth and is always on the verge of laughing himself silly. Then he climbs out of the turtle

PAWAHTUN

shell on his back, which he beats like a drum when he's dancing. The shell is always handy when his mood turns black and he needs a place to hide.

Now either he's unusually tiny or the turtle shell on his back is gigantic. It's hard to believe the Creators chose a creature no bigger than a thumb to support the world forever. Maybe that's the joke that sends Pawahtun into uncontrollable fits of laughter. He may be even smaller than a thumb, because he stuffs a lot of other things inside his shell, like leaves and seeds and young shoots of corn. Pawahtun has another curious habit: he weaves a spiderweb around himself and sometimes lives inside it. He's probably not a man at all.

Whatever he is, he's stronger than a boar's horn, stronger than the seven snakes that weave the rainbow. Either that, or the sky is as light as a feather.

"And speaking of the sky," said Chak. "It needs some rearranging."

The gods pondered the matter. Like every skywatcher, they each had a different opinion, which changed from moment to moment depending on the weather.

"The sky should have nine levels," said the Stingray Paddler. "And each level should weigh as much as a stack of warm tortillas."

"Nine black swarms? That's ridiculous," said the Jaguar Paddler. "Everyone knows our sky has thirteen layers, and these layers resemble the folds in a giant tamale."

"What do they know?" said Pawahtun. "The sky is a bluebird and a crow. The sky is a starry cage and a basket of clouds."

Pawahtun has the soul of a poet, and while he was lost in thought, the gods picked up their chisels and created a sky that looked like a large stone throne weighing fifty tons.

"Help!" said Pawahtun. "Don't you know the sky is a blue water lily floating on the surface of the Underworld sea?"

The most divine artists disagreed. They painted the sky as a sublime blue wave rippling through the air, the palest moonlit shadow no heavier than a thought.

PAWAHTUN

"Delete that," said Pawahtun. "The sky is a clam, a silver squid, a baby lizard sleeping in my turban."

Gods with wilder imaginations made a sky that looked like a mean crocodilian sort of snake with long claws and deer's ears and a hunched back big enough to carry the sun, moon, stars, and planets on its immense body. Sad to say, this Sky Serpent, this Cosmic Dragon, this Starry Deer Alligator had no tail. Instead, the monster had two heads, one in front and one in back. Rain poured down from its double jaws, bringing double floods or double blessings.

"Have it your way," Pawahtun shrugged. "Tortillas, corn cakes, blue waves, deer snakes: these strange pictures of the sky are no big problem for a clever little fellow like me."

If the sky should form an enormous square, Pawahtun just splits himself in four, and each one holds up a corner.

"Good to see you again," he says to himself. "And you and you and you."

But if the sky turns into a ball, the four Pawahtuns get into serious trouble, bumping and rolling all around heaven.

"Ooof, that was my elbow, you bumbler!"

"Kindly remove your bony finger from my eye."

"Please take your toe out of my ear, you insufferable, lopsided cloud chaser."

"Hmm, I must write down that insult and save it for a special occasion," Pawahtun mutters after he pulls himself together. "There's a certain perverse poetry in that line. But those artists, why don't they make up their minds? Those spiral designs make me dizzy!"

When the Sky Serpent wiggles, it throws Pawahtun off balance. Streaking comets cause a stabbing pain in his right knee. In the rainy season, the sky feels like a gigantic bag of water. In the dry season, the sky twitches like a field of hungry grasshoppers. The stars don't seem to weigh any more than the light of a thousand candles, but the sun burns his shoulders, the moon stirs his memories, the clouds twist his thoughts. "What are the stars made of and what does it mean?" he wonders.

"And the immense spaces in between the stars? Is my eyesight getting weaker or is the night sky a huge black mirror?" So many questions, so few answers. "I'm not a physicist," he cries and crawls into his shell.

"No room to think. No room to count. No room to write my couplets. Impossible to make any sense when I'm just me, myself, and I."

That's when the sky trembles and the world begins to sob.

"If only the sky were a beautiful woman who would keep me warm on winter nights."

When he moves his hand to wipe away the tears he feels the planets start to slip into the sea. "Oops! Don't let go of the serpent throne ball," he sighs. "Hold on, old man, hold on."

He's always on the verge of laughing himself silly. Then he climbs out of the turtle shell on his back, which he beats like a drum when he's dancing.

TEZCATLIPOCA
LORD of
the SMOKING MIRROR

T he noiselessness is sudden, a heavy door closing on the storm. Few who enter that silent land return. There is no trace of human life in the valleys or on the barren hills. There is no draft, no murmur, no sound of footsteps, no chink of stone, no breath.

This stillness is the birthplace of fanged toads, feathered serpents, lizards with flowering tongues. They survive as *naguales*, animal spirits, of the gods of rain and night.

A pool the size of the moon is said to form in the sand at the time of the full moon, and from its depths rises a plume of smoke dim as obsidian. The smoke, people say, is the essence of Tezcatlipoca, Lord of the Smoking Mirror, god of magic and invisibility.

In the plume of smoke, wanderers see their souls in the shapes of birds, red ants, or dogs. Immediately they take flight or crawl beneath the ocotillo cactuses. Some turn into needles waiting for water. Others turn into lightning stones or jagged flints. Others change into black shadows, unable to escape, unable to will themselves awake, locked like their god on the dark side of the mirror. This is the land of loss where everything takes its bleakest form, forged in smoke, hammered in silence.

There was a time when Tezcatlipoca created fire. There was a time when he defeated the Earth Monster that haunted the bottom of the sea. But after he lost his foot, the crippled hero grew despondent, and he remained bitter and brokenhearted long after his foot turned into a smoking mirror. For centuries he brooded over his right foot. For centuries he stared into the smoking mirror, and little by little, he discovered that the mirror gave him the power to see the future. At last he saw his fate. Tezcatlipoca became the black night wind. No one could hear or see him.

Tezcatlipoca flew to the east and wrestled with his brother, Ehecatl, the god of benevolent winds. So deep were their differences, so violent their quarrels, that four times they tore the world apart and four times they put it back together—so thick was their bond as brothers, so loyal to the everlasting earth and its good and evil souls.

Tezcatlipoca traveled south, and when he reached the land of the Maya he saw a miniature version of himself on the opposite side of an obsidian mirror. Here was a

Tezcatlipoca traveled south,
and when he reached
the land of the Maya
he saw a miniature version
of himself
on the opposite side
of an obsidian mirror.

god of wind, lightning, and fire who wore a smoking mirror on his forehead and whose right leg turned into a snake. This precious one, Kawil, ruled the divine spark within the blood. He, too, was mysterious, silent, and invisible as he brought forth abundant crops and fruits and guided the fortunes of kings. "Why would I harm my shadow?" Tezcatlipoca thought.

When Tezcatlipoca reached the Pacific Ocean, he met another god of wind named Ik. Though he lived by the sea, his power was surprisingly gentle. All this happened so long ago that Ik hadn't thought of causing a stir or raising a storm or hurting a pebble. He moved about like a spirit, breathing the breath of life into all the earth's creatures. Tezcatlipoca, the night wind, was completely disarmed.

No one hears the sound of Tezcatlipoca's sunken step. But listen. At night you may hear the moonlight land on a leaf or a shadow brush an owl's wing. If you hear the deepening tone of a bow drawn slowly across the bass string of a cello, it is the low vibration of the planets crossing heaven. That weary moan is Our Mother Earth turning in her sleep. That distant drumbeat is the god fanning the winds of war.

Tezcatlipoca draws the night to him like a magnet. At dawn he is the blue hummingbird stirring up chaos. The delicate note you hear is the sound of his silver flute setting the blinding sun on his path.

Tezcatlipoca is everywhere. He is the wind that keeps the world spinning between daylight and darkness.

4
SUPERNATURAL
SERPENTS

WHEN SNAKES RULED THE WORLD

4
SUPERNATURAL
SERPENTS

Back in the time of shadows when the earth was a nervous monster—rumbling and lumbering and shaking mountains and all the creatures that crawled or swam— serpents ruled the world. Yes, their dreadful fangs could bite, cause sickness and even death. But snakes possessed one awesome feature. They were able to shed their skins, and this gave them magical powers of transformation.

Hanging in the trees, they became the living jeweled branches. Rocks were black stone serpents that had fallen into deep and wondrous sleep. The hills were restless green serpents rolling toward the plains.

Springs bursting forth from the earth were blue snakes that appeared in the form of water. Rivers rippled with their undulating motion. When the rains came, people would never think of saying, "It's raining cats and dogs." They'd say it was pouring crystal snakes the size of teardrops.

Oh, it makes you shiver, but not as much as lightning streaking

across the sky in the shape of a silver serpent whose crackling tail could split the heavens. On clear nights, people looked up and saw an immense serpent made of stars. On clear days they gazed at pale serpents curling in the clouds, or gray snakes rising from the smoke of cooking fires.

In the Age of Serpents, snakes filled the thoughts and dreams of people whose minds possessed a reptilian sliver, which sometimes made them behave like snakes. The slow, mellifluous voice of the talking serpent echoed in every song and story. Short or long, diamond-backed or striped, serpents were the rainbow and the fire.

SAVED
from the
HORNED SERPENT

here was a rock with horns. The rock moved and the rock spoke. "My name is Xul Vo' Ton," said the rock. "There is a Horned Serpent living underneath me. It comes out on Wednesdays and

Thursdays. He plows up the earth with his horns."

It was true. Every Wednesday and Thursday a beautiful spring flowed from the rock.

The spring was the path of the snake.

Perhaps it was their singing, perhaps it was their laughter, but when people came to live beside the spring, the earth trembled. The sky trembled. The Horned Serpent wrapped himself around the clouds and brought terrible storms and floods.

When he shook his horns and tunneled deep inside the earth, the rivers sank and the streams refused to bubble. The cornfields became dry canyons. The people wrung their hands.

And so they prayed to the rock.

"The land is quaking. The rivers are sinking. We're dying of thirst."

"Thank you for praying to me," said the rock. "I will hide the Horned Serpent. He won't be shaking the earth anymore."

Then Thunderbolt hurled his lightning. He knocked the horns off the rock.

The people have plenty of water now. Every May they clean the spring and hold a celebration. If no one leaves food for the Horned Serpent, he will cause earthquakes, famine, and floods.

The
SERPENT
of FIRE

Once there was a proud king who was making the rounds of his vast kingdom. Disguised as a poor peasant, he traveled from village to village, visiting his people to learn their innermost thoughts.

One evening he came to the door of an old widow. "Come in, come in," she said. "I have no food, I have no drink. I have nothing to offer but the comfort of my fire."

The fire was dancing cheerfully, and the king was happy to rest by the old woman's hearth. After a while he noticed that the old crone never added wood to the fire and yet it continued to burn.

"The smoke carries my prayers to heaven," the old woman said. "Despite the selfishness of our king, I have all I need."

Bathed in the warm glow of the fire, the king simmered down and soon dropped off to sleep. When he awoke the next morning, the fire was blazing under the woman's tortilla griddle. It smoldered under her bean pot all day and flared up again at night.

"Your fire changes by itself, old

The Fire Serpent

bared its red fangs and

became the Serpent of War.

The king fought with flaming arrows,

obsidian knives, and lightning bolts.

His enemies were helpless.

woman. How do you do it?" asked the king.

"My fire is a living thing," she said, "as old as time and the sun. It's magic. And the magic is for me alone."

The king couldn't help himself. He wanted to own the fire and began plotting to take it away.

"I know who you are and I know what you are thinking. If you steal this fire, your kingdom will perish and you will lose everything," the old woman croaked. "*Krrik, krrik!*" And with that, she turned into a toucan and flew to the rafters of her thatched hut.

The angry king picked up the woman's ladle and swatted the rebellious bird. It fell down dead. Immediately he pulled off the bird's yellow bill, scooped up the fire, and fled into the night. When he reached his palace, the fire was humming and hissing inside the toucan's orange beak.

Once it came into his possession, the fire became fierce and wild. The king placed the fire on the tip of his royal

The SERPENT of FIRE

scepter, but his turquoise scepter turned into a torch and then a serpent with flaming scales.

Soon the serpent escaped and began eating everything in its path—wood, grass, cornfields, and forests. Fire split the stones of the palace and turned the king's jade jewels to ash. Neither the blue lakes nor wide rivers could quench the fire's fury. The kingdom was white with cinders, and the seething Fire Serpent could not be tamed.

The king beat his fists until they were bloody. "My enemies have sent this curse," he boiled. "I will arm myself and slay them all!"

The Fire Serpent bared its red fangs and became the Serpent of War. The king fought with flaming arrows, obsidian knives, and lightning bolts. His enemies were helpless.

"Now I will fight fire with fire," said the enraged king, and he went off to battle the volcanoes. The mountains steamed and smoked and spewed hot lava, but again the king was victorious because the Fire Serpent was the lord of volcanoes and burning blazes. The land was utterly destroyed.

"Now I will challenge the Lord of the Sun," bragged the king. But the Fire Serpent was the spear of the sun, and the king was consumed in its flames.

In time he returned to the world as a poor wood gatherer, and despite his miserable poverty, he found a wife, who sold tamales in the market. She cooked them over the few twigs he gathered in the blackened forest. "The serpent needs feeding," she'd say, and off he'd go. He was just a servant now, with soot on his hands and soot on his brow and a wife who nagged him if the fire died down. The man who was once a king spent the rest of his life doing the work of a woman, feeding the hungry Fire Serpent coiled up in the hearth.

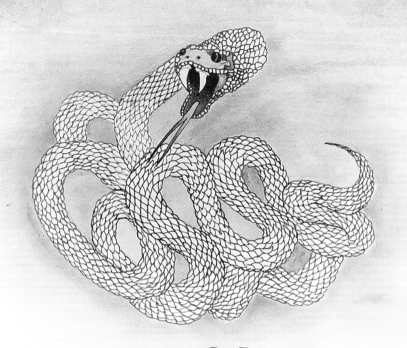

The CLOUD SERPENT

 hite as snow, black as crows, drifting on a slow wind or shrouding the face of the sun, the Cloud Serpent has as many shapes and moods as the greatest gods. He may start as a

small puff of a bird and billow into a creature you've never seen before—something resembling a white-tailed deer with eagle wings or a five-legged monster from the black bog thirteen worlds below this world. This shape-shifting is for sheer pleasure.

The Cloud Serpent also leaves mysterious signs in the sky—wispy lines and isosceles triangles—and then . . . erases them with a sigh. These signs are sent to us as gifts and omens.

Once a great Chichimec hunter lifted his eyes from the swirling dust of the northern desert and saw a silver arrow speed across the sky. He changed his name to Mixcoatl, "Cloud Serpent," and led his scruffy warriors south in search of better game. In the Valley of Mexico he saw cloudlike palaces adorned with crystal gems. In the misty mountains of Oaxaca he met the "Cloud People," the Mixtecs, who decorated their temples with the diamond designs of the Cloud Serpent. In the red land of the Maya, he came face to face with the giant dragon whose steaming scales dissolved in smoky S's. How could he battle a moving cloud?

Mixcoatl knew his winding path through life made similar patterns—S's, zigzags, and stepped frets leading up to the thirteenth sky. At the end of his days, he climbed the steps as if they were a ladder, and there in the clouds the hunter became a god and the father of the gods of wind.

At night the Cloud Serpent races across the moon on his way to the upper heavens. There he changes into a cloud of stars, the Milky Way. The Cloud Serpent is a maker of dreams, people say, dreams, like white-tailed deer, that are always fleeting.

The
VISION
SERPENT

S ome serpents live on the earth, others dwell in the sky. The Vision Serpent easily moves from one level of the universe to another. Though this serpent is made of clouds and fire, he can slip beneath the blood-red sea and down the snakelike passages of the Underworld. There he watches and listens.

The souls of ordinary folk, who slave in the fields and the kitchens, are groaning and weeping and praying for release. The souls of nobles do nothing but reminisce about their glorious feats, outdoing one another with tales of victorious battles, the victims they slew, the visions they dreamed, the cities they built, the rains they brought, the books they wrote, the games they won, the drinks they served, the astronomers they paid, the poets they entertained, the profound happiness of their subjects. They have the scars and jewels and sharp minds to prove it, though neither wounds nor wealth nor wisdom will relieve their sorrow or buy their escape.

The Lords of Death just sit around the fire, warming their bones and chuckling about yesterday's disasters and today's message of doom, which the owls deliver without delay from the surface of the earth. Occasionally it's possible to pick up a little tidbit about something that will happen tomorrow. The Vision Serpent possesses secret knowledge about the past, and the Vision Serpent sees the future. Of all the supernatural snakes in snakedom, he is the most spiritual.

Most people must be content to communicate with their ancestors once a year, on the Day of the Dead, when the souls come up to eat and drink with their families. Once a year was not enough for ancient kings and queens, who had to contend with rebellions, wars, droughts, and other delicate matters of state. They needed to know the future in a hurry. Their calendar keepers foretold events by interpreting the omens attached to each day. Other diviners read the stars; still others listened to birdcalls. But as anyone could tell you, if you want good advice, the best thing to do is ask a snake. Not just any snake, of course. "THE snake! The one down there."

Out of the bowl

he rose like a tortured wave,

rearing and hissing,

higher and higher.

The trouble was, very few were brave enough to go all the way down to the Underworld for a brief conversation. The rapids might swallow you, the clashing mountains crush you, the stone benches burn your seat. The Lords of Death would try to snatch you, lock you in the House of Knives or the House of Cold. Old Jaguar Foot would smile and serve you tamales and the next minute cut off your head. No, it was a perilous business, and only the divine twins, Hunapu and Xbalanque, were clever enough to survive the dangers.

After much thought and careful practice, the kings and queens devised a method for summoning the Vision Serpent. It was not easy.

They began by stripping off their jade ornaments, their brocaded robes, and like the hermits who roamed the wilderness, covered their nakedness with soot. Freed of riches, emptied of pride, they descended to the dingy labyrinths beneath the palace or retreated to remote mountain caves. There they fasted and prayed to the spirit of lightning,

the spirit of fire. When they emerged from the dank subterranean vaults after days and nights of penance, they were so weak they could barely stand and their minds were half-crazed. They had seen all sorts of terrifying things in the pitch black, and they had felt the pulse of the blue snake that coursed through their royal blood. They were priests now, powerful shamans. Exalted, they entered the holy sanctuary of the temple and offered their blood. The precious drops of royal blood fell on strips of paper lying in a bowl, and the spattered paper was set on fire. The smoke and the serpent in the blood summoned the Vision Serpent.

Out of the bowl he rose like a tortured wave, rearing and hissing, higher and higher. Lady Xok, the great queen of Yaxchilan, trembled as the serpent grazed her shoulder and hovered in the fetid air above her head. He hummed and clicked like a lightning bolt and smelled of burning hair. And then he opened his mouth to speak. Between his cavernous jaws and pointed teeth appeared the spirit of an ancient ruler fully armed with a message.

To this day we do not know what the Vision Serpent told her. We do not know if the spirit sang or spoke directly to the woman's heart. We only have a picture of this huge snake writhing up from the Underworld to deliver a message within a message. But the message that was so urgent then is lost. Something about a future battle, something wrong that needed righting. We'll never know this revelation from the gods. That is the nature of visions, so electrifying when they come, so quick to fade in the clouds.

TALES of the PLUMED SERPENT

O f all the many divine snakes, none is more magnificent and revered than the Plumed Serpent. Thanks to his iridescent feathers, this amazing rattlesnake can fly. Where did he come from? How can it be?

Well, he was changing his skin one spring, about a million years ago, when the usually sultry weather turned surprisingly cold. He was all curled up and bare naked, just shivering and trying to keep his wits from freezing over. "Hmmm, I wish I had some warm feathers to ward off this wintry chill, this sudden nip in the tropical air," he murmured. And by the incredible powers that even young gods possess, he imme-diately sprouted feathers from head to tail.

Old women will tell you the clever rattlesnake coaxed the female quetzal bird into lending him her long, resplendent feathers. He couldn't help but notice how her long tail undulated like a serpent as she flew through the cloud forest. "We'll make a handsome pair," he said. "You're far too ugly, you mud-sopped creature," she said, "but at

least my gorgeous train will cover up those rough scales and noisy rattles." Her loyal mate protested, calling from the branches, calling from the hills, but she was a generous spirit and it was too late. She shook and shimmied and the feathers flew. They covered the snake's body from head to tail until he was iridescent. And he could fly!

People who despise talking snakes and talking birds, no matter how smart and handsome, are certain the Plumed Serpent came from the dreams of devils. "Surely this marvelous serpent is a creature of black magic," they insist, pointing their finger at the old sorcerer, Itzamna. "He is the kind of god who would dream of such things, being some sort of snake bird himself."

Those who worship the Plumed Serpent for his great gifts of wizardry believe he was born from his own thoughts and sprang into this world fully feathered and flying.

He flies over the cloud forests of the Maya highlands, over the jungles, over the swamps. He circles above Mexico City. He flies over the deserts of the Southwest and up the Mississippi. He is known by many different names—*Kukulcan* by the Maya, *Quetzalcoatl* by the Aztecs, *Kolowisi* among the Zuni, *Palalukong* by the Hopi.

Everywhere he goes, the Plumed Serpent is honored as the guardian of water. He is also the living cord that connects the earth and the Underworld. Wherever he appears, the Plumed Serpent is worshipped as a god and savior. Because he travels far and wide, there are hundreds of different stories about him, and all of them are true.

Once upon a time, the Plumed Serpent was a water spirit that came from the sea when there was nothing but the sea, silent, dark, and rippling. There was only a pale glittering light ruffling his blue-green feathers as he floated in the middle of the sea, his blue-green feathers the color of the waters, when he and the god of thunderbolts started talking. They

Everywhere he goes,

the Plumed Serpent

is honored as the

guardian of water.

He is also

the living cord that

connects the earth and

the Underworld.

talked and thought and worried and then talked some more, and finally they decided how they would create the world. They did it with their words and ringing voices, as some say Itzamna had done.

The mountains, streams, and cypress trees came about as they had planned, but the animals, insects, and birds disturbed the gods with their endless racket. So the gods decided to create humans. The potters made them out of clay. But the people of clay just melted and turned into mud.

"A-h-h-h, this g-g-g-od aren't soo g-g-g-rit," said the next race of people. But what did they know? They were made out of wooden sticks. They had no minds or souls and could barely speak. They had no respect for the gods. And so jaguars ate them; fires, winds, and floods destroyed them. The gods tried again and again.

The Plumed Serpent was getting more and more exasperated. You see, he had four sides to his nature, and not all of them were nice.

"He can't be all good," said his brother. And who was his brother? The sly, one-footed, magical god of night, Tezcat-lipoca, the Smoking Mirror. The two of them started squabbling right away. From then on, the brothers took turns remaking the world and then destroying everything on it. It seemed that human beings never turned out right.

In a mood of melancholy, the Plumed Serpent changed into the wind. Ehecatl looked like a duck with a long red beak. Whenever he took a deep breath he sounded like a whistling toad. Around his neck he wore a conch shell, to remind him of the sea. His beautiful "wind jewel" came from the Underworld. This is how it happened.

After the floods destroyed the world, people were transformed into fish and their thin bones sank to the bottom of the dreary Underworld sea. First Ehecatl and Tezcatlipoca struggled and strained and lifted the earth from the waters. Then they turned into trees and raised the sky. By that time the two brothers were worn out, and they still had the job of creating new and better people. So they sat on a rock and thought and thought, and finally Ehecatl said, "They will be made of ground-up bones mixed with our divine blood."

Accompanied by his faithful dog, Ehecatl went down to the Underworld and gathered up all the bones of humankind.

"Not so fast!" growled the Lord of Death. "Those bones belong to me!" Ehecatl begged and pleaded, but the Lord of Death just shook his head, "Not till my eyeballs turn to ice! Certainly not! No way!"

Ehecatl remained as calm as a summer breeze, and after a while the Lord of Death thought of a way to have some fun with him. "I will give you the bones if you can blow this conch shell trumpet," he said. The trouble was, the shell had no holes, and even the wind god couldn't blow it.

Ehecatl whistled for the ants. They swarmed from the rotten trees, they marched in single file from their nests, and when they arrived, Ehecatl asked them, "Please bore holes in this conch for me." Well, their tiny jaws ate away at the shell, and the holes were made in a min-ute. Ehecatl blew the conch shell trumpet, and the deep blast shook every corner and crevice of the Underworld caves. Ehecatl scooped up the bones and ran.

The Lord of Death was completely rat-tled. Clinking and clanging, he scuttled up and down the tunnels, chasing after the god of wind. Ehecatl kept running, but just as he reached the door, he dropped some of the bones, and they cracked and broke on the rocks. That's why human beings come in different sizes, short, medium, and tall.

Ehecatl rushed to Tamoanchan, the Land of Mists, and there the bones were ground to a fine meal. Then the gods add-ed a few drops of their blood and a bit of spit for good measure. Out of this mixture, new men and women were created. From then on, Ehecatl brought the rains that watered the fields and fruit trees, raised the corn, and took care of all living things.

One day the Plumed Serpent was circling above one of his temples. The temple was as round as his cone-shaped hat, round as a serpent's coils, round as the wind. Around and around he flew, and on his third round, he accidently swallowed a feather. He burped, and a full-grown man emerged from his mouth. The man had pale skin, a long red beard, and his face looked like a broken stone. His name was Topiltzin.

Topiltzin became the great and wise rul-er of Tula. He taught the Toltec people the arts of sculpture, featherwork, and writ-ing. He built temples of jade, turquoise, and coral. There was nothing he couldn't do. Although he was a king, he lived as a poor priest dedicated to worshipping the Plumed Serpent. He forbade human sac-rifice and instead offered butterflies and flowers to the gods. The gods must have been pleased because the cotton grew in red, blue, yellow, green, and a hundred other colors; the squashes were as big as melons; the corn was the size of a man's arm. Everything Topiltzin did was good, and his kingdom was the most glorious on earth.

Only one god was displeased with the good fortunes of the people, and that was the jealous Tezcatlipoca. The sorcerer cast a spell that drove the Toltecs into a mad frenzy. He tempted Topiltzin with wine and beautiful women and led the holy king astray.

In shame, Topiltzin burned his beautiful palaces, abandoned Tula, and set off for the east. He crossed jagged mountain peaks, plodded over sharp volcanic rocks and drifts of freezing snow. He walked the jungle trails in sorrow. At the great Maya city of Chichen Itza, home of the Plumed Serpent, Kukulkan, he lingered for a while, filling the dry water holes before moving on. Finally he reached the shores of the Gulf of Mexico. There he made a raft of braided snakes and drifted out to sea. From north, south, east, and west came flocks of many-colored birds. They filled the swirling air with brightness as they lifted the serpent raft, twist-ing and curling, into the sky. And in the blinding light of dawn, Topiltzin turned into the morning star.

Lamat, the great star known as Venus, has many guises. He is a fair-haired man whose pale skin changes to feathered scales at sunrise. He wears two finny fish barbels at the corners of his mouth. He limps on one leg like a rain bird. He was born from a stone on the day Nine Wind, and he is the wind. His home is a shell in the sea. He bathes in the pure waters of the Milky Way. Rising before dawn, he is the faithful servant who sweeps the path of the sun. Rising at dusk, he follows his companion, the sundog, and his brother, Lord of Night. Later, when the heavens are pricked with needles of light, he dives underground. For months he wanders through the Underworld, invisible as a ghost, restless as moonlight. Then he reappears at dawn, red as the sun, and becomes master of war and destruc-tion. Venus is the planet of the Plumed Serpent, and like the Plumed Serpent, he is the great god of change.

The HORRIBLE
WHITE BONE
CENTIPEDE

O h, this one's a twister, all black and blue and covered with blisters. Seven black tongues loll in each of her seven heads. Ten red eyes glare from the tips of her claws. She has a body made of pig snouts and shark fins for feet.

The HORRIBLE WHITE BONE CENTIPEDE

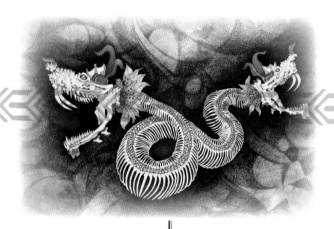

Her ratty hair is a tangled web of tarantula spiders. You'd better get out of town or run to the other side of the street, though it won't save you from her steaming spit. Of course, she's covered with spines and quills. Buzzard feathers fly from her mouth when she squeaks. When she catches you in her coils she sucks the breath from your nose, and absolutely nothing can save you. No one knows who dreamed her up, but she is older than dreams, older than the slimy mud she lives under, croaking curses like the awful night she was born.

Ugly as she is, she has a terrible older brother. Of all the weird, scaly, winged, hairy, stinking creatures that inhabit the Underworld, he is the creepiest.

White Bone Centipede, by name, looks like the skeleton of a long-dead snake, but don't let that fool you. He has a hundred greasy legs that crawl faster than you can run. He waits like some moldy, rotten, chewed-up thing at the entrances to caves. He *is* the mouth of caves, because his gaping jaws are so huge. Anyone who slips through the cracks of his bucktoothed fangs sticks to the insides of his wormy body, all slick white armor and goo. There's no way out because he is the son of Death. Bone is the rattle of his breath and everlasting is his poisonous sting.

White Bone
Centipede

by name,

looks like the skeleton

of a long-dead snake,

but don't let that fool you.

He has a hundred

greasy legs that crawl faster

than you can run.

The WATER LILY JAGUAR

ater Lily Jaguar swims in the silver rivers of the rainforest. Water Lily Jaguar swims in the silver pool of the moon.

When waves of lily pads tremble and heave, you know the Water Lily Jaguar is

swimming underwater, searching for tasty catfish. When he comes up for air, he will be dripping in water lily flowers, water lily vines, from head to toe. If he doesn't rise to the surface, he has dived deeper, down to the bottom of the bottomless lagoon, down through the sunless caverns, down to the sunless palace where the Lords of Death are having supper.

Water Lily Jaguar marches,

Water Lily Jaguar prowls the halls sniffing for something to eat. There is nothing on the fire but stacks of burning bones, nothing to drink but jugs full of blood. Next time one of those dreadful lords—Pus Master or Bone Scepter—says something nasty, he may have to take a nibble. But the Lords of Death never speak crossly to Water Lily Jaguar. They show him great respect, not simply because

he is fierce, but because
he is a terrific dancer.

When Water Lily Jaguar
prances, the eyeballs on his
necklace jangle, the bells clang on his
tail. When Water Lily Jaguar dances, water lily petals sweeten the air as he spins.
His coat of stars is sending out sparks, his
golden fur is flashing rays of light.

Oh, he is really whirling now, and the
Lords of Death are beating their turtle
shell drums and pounding their feet.
They're shuffling and stumbling and tot-
tering in circles, banging and crashing and
crunching each other's toes. The kings
are wearing their high-backed sandals and
stomping on the stones.

And now they're all coming out of the
woodwork, the knife bats and fish flies
and two-headed geeks. The footless

birds and spiny worms are
delighted there's a party.

The crabs and the lizards are
waltzing up a storm. The music is
getting louder now because the anteat-
ers are blowing their trumpets. And who's
that hairy frog tooting on his horn?

And who's that coming here and steaming up the room? Why it's the Sun, Our
Father, dancing with Grandmother Moon!
And isn't that Venus leading the snake
dance with the lightning-footed god of
storms? And isn't that the Night Wind
doing the one-step all alone?

The dance floor is thundering with hoof
beats and claws. The air is reeling with
glass wings, dog stinks, and buzzing anten-
nae. Things get out of hand when Water
Lily Jaguar dances, and the dead start
jumping for joy.

THE MAYA

A Brief History

One day, in 1746, a twelve-year-old Mexican boy named José de la Fuente Coronado was wandering through the jungle near Palenque when he came upon the mossy walls of what appeared to be a palace. Its abandoned rooms were thick with vines, the empty corridors adorned with solemn faces, figures, and rows of strange beasts. Temples crowned the surrounding hills, but on closer inspection, the hills were not hills at all; they were giant pyramids with stone steps leading upward. The boy spoke and dreamed of nothing else, and soon word of this enchanted place spread throughout the region. When news of the lost city reached the king of Spain, the mysteries of the ancient stones captured the world's imagination.

Who built those magnificent pyramids? Who were those godlike figures carved in stone? What did their strange hieroglyphic writing say?

After a century of exploration, we know that the ancestors of the Maya people living near the ruins today built those spectacular cities over two thousand years ago. The faces carved on the temples are images of gods or portraits of divine kings and queens, and the writing on the walls celebrates the extraordinary history of one of the greatest civilizations in the New World.

The stones speak of deeper mysteries: the nature of the cosmos, of

space and time. For the Maya, this creation began on August 13, 3114 B.C. From that date they counted millions of days back to past creations and millions of days into the distant future. The Long Count Calendar was endless, bigger than the universe!

Time also moved in shorter cycles: the 819-day calendar; the 260-day sacred calendar; the Venus cycle; the lunar series; and the Nine Lords of Night, who ruled over the nine hours of darkness. With so many cycles of time, it's a wonder the calendar priests could keep track, but they did, counting the days and observing the orbits of the sun, moon, and planets almost as accurately as scientists today. Accuracy was important for

predicting eclipses, knowing the proper time for planting, and for divining individual destinies. People and gods were often named for the day on which they were born. The Calendar Round foretold events in everyday life and gave a circular pattern to Maya history.

In the *Books of Chilam Balam*, the Jaguar Priests wrote that time began when a divine being who looked very much like a man set his footprint on the road. Nobody knows when that happened, but the journey was hard and long.

The *Popol Vuh*, the great epic of the K'iche Maya people, tells us that the ancestors came to the New World by following seven stepping-pingstones across the sea. Some scientists say that the first Americans traveled from Asia in boats over 16,000 years ago. When they landed along the Pacific coast, they enjoyed a prosperous life as fishermen, eating shrimp and clams to their heart's content and piling the shells into giant mounds that still stand among the mangrove swamps of southern Mexico.

Eventually the Maya migrated into the lush mountains of Guatemala. Then, about 4000 years ago, they started walking south to Honduras and El Salvador, east to Belize and the Yucatan Peninsula, west to Chiapas, and as far north as the Huasteca area of Veracruz. In these humid, volcanic regions they planted corn, built houses of mud and thatch, and settled down. Over time they learned to survive earthquakes, torrential storms, and searing heat, all the perils of two opposing times of year, the rainy season and the dry. Only two civilizations have flourished in the jungle. Like the Khmer of Cambodia,

the Maya saw life as a balance of opposites: light and dark, birth and death, abundance and desolation. The idea must have come from observing the cycles of nature.

Once the Maya settled down, their world changed dramatically. During the Preclassic period (1500–100 B.C.), they began making fine pottery and building stone structures decorated with images of the divine bird Seven Macaw. Their small villages swelled into city-states and their temples grew into manmade mountains. The great center of El Mirador was populated by more than fifty thousand people, and its main pyramid rose 230 feet above the jungle floor. At the top of the social pyramid stood the king (*ahaw*), who ruled over the nine levels of the Underworld and thirteen levels of the sky.

Prosperity rested on the sweat of the corn farmers as well as the cleverness of Maya merchants. These adventurous men never stopped walking the roads, becoming part of a vast trading network that put them in touch with the material and intellectual riches of other Mesoamerican cultures. From the Zoques living along the Pacific coast they learned the story of the Hero Twins. From their Olmec neighbors on the Gulf of Mexico, they acquired rubber and mirrors along with mathematics, astronomy, and writing. By 250 B.C. the Maya developed their own unique system of hieroglyphic writing, which was composed of pictures and symbols that represented spoken syllables.

For unknown reasons, cities like El Mirador were abandoned in 100 B.C. and people moved to other areas of the rainforest. That period is known as the Preclassic collapse.

The low point in the cycle didn't last long because the Maya brought their knowledge, languages, and customs with them and started building large cities again. Now they were carving their history in stone, recording the names and dates of their rulers as well as the names and dates of their enemies, some as far away as Teotihuacan, near modern Mexico City. During the Classic period (A.D. 200–900), Maya civilization came into full flower.

There were hundreds of centers in the Maya realm competing for political, economic, and religious power. Despite their glorious achievements, none of the great city-states—Palenque, Tikal, Calakmul, and Copan—was able to form a unified empire.

Instead, art, science, and religion united the independent city-states. Renowned artists and scribes who traveled from city to city established a fairly standard art style and system of writing. Mathematicians and astronomers shared their latest discoveries: the proper geometric proportions of the temples, rare planetary conjunctions, and the precise dates of future solar eclipses. Although each city had its favorite deities and myths, the same gods were worshipped throughout the Maya region.

On festival days, thousands crowded the ceremonial centers to witness a new king take the throne or to observe the end of a calendar cycle. These public spectacles were often staged at the solstices, equinoxes, zenith or nadir passages, when the sun bathed the red temples in dazzling rays of light. During those celebrations, the sky and earth, the physical and spiritual worlds were in harmony.

The many levels of the Maya universe were reflected in the many levels of society. Nobles of the royal courts held sumptuous feasts attended by dancers, drummers, acrobats, and actors dressed in extravagant costumes. While the nobles were busy plotting political intrigues and alliances, the long-distance merchants were seeking precious jades, cottons, cacao, and other luxuries to delight the upper class. Stonecutters polished exquisite jade jewels and carved delicate bas-reliefs for noble houses. The most gifted artisans, often members of the ruling elite, painted fine ceramics to be buried in royal tombs. Meanwhile, potters crafted everyday cookware and figurines for household altars. In the markets, venders traded corn, salt, beans, and chili peppers produced by the farmers.

Although farmers lived on the lowest rung of society, their labors were the most honored. Corn was the foundation of Maya daily life and religion. People were made of corn and therefore part of the natural cycle of life, death, and rebirth. The great cycles of creation, the movements of the stars and planets, were related to the seasonal growth and harvesting of corn from mother earth.

The levels of society, the levels of

the cosmos, and the thirteen parts of the soul were one. Plants, stars, and human destiny were intertwined.

The night sky was a mirror that reflected life in the Underworld. The ancestors who dwelled in the darkness below could be seen as stars at night. They shared the immense sky with Owl, Peccary, Eagle, Jaguar, and other supernatural animals that made up the Maya constellations.

Needless to say, the Maya saw the night sky differently than the Greeks and Romans. Orion's Belt was pictured as a turtle carrying three stars on its back. The turtle also represented the earth. Three other stars in Orion—Mintaka, Saiph, and Rigel—were seen as Three Hearthstones that sit in the center of a Maya house. The Milky Way represented the World Tree, the starry white road to Xibalba, and the giant Crocodile whose upper body formed the heavens.

As for the planets, Venus was envisioned as a feathered serpent as well as a vicious god of war. In other words, something as certain as a star had many identities.

The same was true for people. On the earth's surface, men and women possessed an animal soul that tied them to the natural world. While a person was sleeping, his or her animal soul would wander through the wilderness, and if it were harmed, the person would get sick. Powerful shamans had the animal souls of jaguars and hummingbirds and could transform themselves into these beings at will. The White Bone Centipede was the companion animal spirit of K'an Bahlam, king of Palenque.

Kings and queens lived in luxury, but their duties were many. As gods in human form, they were responsible for maintaining an orderly society in harmony with the agricultural cycle and the great cosmic forces. Adorned in jade ornaments and lavish feathers, they represented the tree of life at the center of the world. As high priests, they had the power to communicate with the gods. In the art of Yaxchilan, the queen, Lady Xok, is seen conversing with the Vision Serpent before her husband goes to war. In order to guarantee continued prosperity, rulers regularly sacrificed their own blood.

Kings and queens were trained warriors expected to do battle. On public monuments they pose in quilted cotton armor, subduing their captives with war shields, clubs, and spears. Kings were also accomplished ballplayers.

Of all the Maya pastimes, none was more popular than the ballgame, *pok-ta-pok*. The game, which resembled soccer, was not just a sport. The rubber ball represented the sun and the ball court was the doorway to the Under-world. When Maya kings played the game, they represented the Hero Twins who defeated the Lords of Death. In order to reenact the story, warriors invaded a nearby kingdom, captured a noble, and after playing the ballgame, sacrificed him to the gods. His bones were considered seeds, and their ritual "planting" promised abundant crops.

Raids on nearby territories eventually turned into long-term struggles between political rivals. Wars, drought, overpopulation, or social unrest threatened the stability of the great city-states. By the ninth century, time completed a circle. Once again the lowland cities were abandoned, and the power shifted to Chichen Itza in the Yucatan Peninsula.

The collapse of Classic Maya civilization marked the end of the rule of divine kings. Yet this ending gave birth to a society dominated by nobles and the wealthy merchant class. As trading networks expanded, more people could acquire the luxuries once reserved for royalty. A simpler art style spread throughout Mesoamerica, along with new ideas and a larger pantheon of gods.

The Postclassic period continued until the Spanish Conquest of 1521. The foreign invaders crushed the ruling class, erased history, and destroyed the writing system. Only four ancient codices survived the Spanish bonfires. The Maya population was decimated.

Five hundred years after the conquest, Maya culture persists. The six million Maya of today speak thirty languages and hundreds of dialects. Of the traditional arts, Maya weavers still produce some of the ancient designs. The living Maya possess an alternate view of the world in which everyday reality and the supernatural coexist and dreams and waking life are interrelated. In some Guatemalan villages, the day keepers maintain the sacred 260-day calendar. Most Maya practice Christianity yet still offer prayers to Chak and remember the gods and goddesses in their stories.

The history of the Maya is a continuing story. With each new archaeological discovery and the decipherment of hieroglyphic texts, we can read another chapter. The Maya developed an enduring civilization in the mountains and rainforests of Mexico and Central America. Their history is part of our past, present, and future.

MAP

of

MESOAMERICA

WEST   NORTH   EAST   SOUTH

MEXICO

Rio Grande

Chichimec Desert

Huasteca Veracruz

Tula

Teotihuacan

Mexico City

VERACRUZ

OAXACA

CHIAPAS

Palenque

Yaxchilan

Bonampak

GUATEMALA

Gulf of Mexico

Chichen Itza

YUCATAN

Calakmul

El Mirador

Tikal

HONDURAS

Copan

EL SALVADOR

Ocean

THE
STORY *of this* BOOK

On my first visit to Palenque, the pyramids were floating through the morning mist like a city in a dream. My friend Moises Morales told me that the dream was real and that if I wanted to understand the ancient Maya I had to spend time in their rainforest world. Soon I was living in a tree house in the jungle where I could barely see the sky through the outstretched arms of ramon trees. Leaves as big as umbrellas sheltered laughing falcons, scarlet macaws, and giant iguanas. At night a lone jaguar, Lord of the Underworld, prowled the hills, howler monkeys roared in the treetops at dawn. Snakes slept in the branches, caimans dozed in the pools, and rooting under the strangler vines were coatis and a wild peccary named Petunia. People spoke of serpent birds, of dwarves with backward feet, of Chak and the guardian spirits who dwelled in caves on San Juan Mountain. The earth was alive and buzzing, dying and coming back to life with every rain. All the creatures around me were characters in the ongoing story of creation.

The story began on a starless night when the earth and sky were wrapped in shadows and the only sound was water rippling. Out of the darkness a woman's voice rose

up and said, "Long ago, when the sky was empty, there was only the sea, only silence, except for a voice rising from the water."

Her words echoed around a thousand campfires centuries before the start of the Long Count Calendar and the first stone temples dedicated to the gods of sun, wind, rain, and lightning. Storytellers knew in their hearts that words were stronger than stones. After all, Itzamna had created the world with his words. Children who rolled with laughter when they heard how the Hero Twins turned their older brothers into monkeys believed every word. After countless tellings, grandmothers dreamed that their stories would outlast the grandest temples, and their dream came

true. With the help of the divine writers Itzamna, Rabbit, Howler Monkey, and Spider Monkey, the Maya became one of five civilizations in the world that devised a written language, not to keep accounts, as the Sumerians and Egyptians did, but to enchant listeners with the deeds of divine kings and queens and the supernatural beings who shaped their world.

Of all the amazing stories poets wrote and recited, only a few exist in a form most of us can read. We know the ancient deities from pictures carved in stone or painted on clay pots, stucco walls, and the pages of hieroglyphic books made of bark paper. The earliest images of the Hero Twins, the Corn God, Chak, and the Feathered Serpent date to 100 BC. The four hiero-glyphic books that survived the Spanish Conquest were written almost a thousand years ago.

It has taken years for scholars to recognize the major gods, mainly by their jaguar spots or serpent legs, crooked noses or swirling eyes. Although a few goddesses have wrinkles or a tail, most look like beautiful young women. Their eternal charms disguise their secret powers as warriors, midwives, and weavers of fate.

There's an even bigger problem for scholars, and that is deciphering the hieroglyphic names of the dei-ties. At first, the gods were assigned letters, A to S. The Lord of the Underworld, for example, became widely known as God L. Recent-ly the epigrapher Michael Grofe identified his name as *B'olon Yokte'* ("Jaguar are his Feet"). For this book, I decided to call him "Old Jaguar Foot."

As for Rabbit (*Tʂul*), he is usually depicted as a writer, though he is often seen snuggling in the arms of a young moon goddess. Rabbit is certainly moonstruck and sly, and for his wicked behavior the gods tossed him on the moon. If you look up at the next full moon, you will see him facing left, with his long floppy ears drooping to the right.

The story about Rabbit stealing Death's fantastic owl hat comes from a scene painted on a clay jar called the Royal Rabbit Vase. Nasty words are pouring out of Rabbit's mouth, and those words are written in the hieroglyphs above Rabbit's head. Poor Old Jaguar Foot is left speechless and shivering.

Imagine puzzling over a hi-eroglyph—a picture made up of sounds—or gazing at a great work of art and trying to figure out what it says. Discovering the words and the story in the picture requires dedicated detective work.

Short, long, magical, or funny, the stories come in snippets that have to be pieced together. Sometimes scholars find missing details in other languages, other places, and other times. The peoples of Mesoamerica have been sharing their gods, and the stories about them, for eons.

So it was that certain Maya myths found eager listeners among the cultures of Oaxaca, central Mexico, and the distant American Southwest. Over thousands of miles and thousands of years, storytellers not only changed the names of deities, but also invented brand new episodes that made the stories more exciting. The tales spread like seeds on the wind, blossoming in dozens of varieties across the Mesoamerican landscape. During the Spanish Conquest, sixteenth-century Aztec

princes told their stories to foreign priests. Of course, the friars added a few ingredients of their own as they rendered the Aztec versions into Spanish. This is why the Plumed Serpent, Kukulcan, became famous under his Aztec name Quetzalcoatl. The same is true for Tezcatlipoca, who shared many traits with the older Maya god Kawil. Both wore magic mirrors and had powers over royal blood and fire. Yet Kawil was overshadowed, largely because the Maya didn't leave behind lengthy songs and stories about their great deity.

No one dared to change a thing about the Earth Monster. Yet the Cloud Serpent drifted from place to place without a firm identity, one minute a pale Maya dragon, the next, a hunter, and then the Milky Way. The streaming cloud of stars that is our galaxy was also seen as a mirrored tree, the white road to Xibalba, the brilliant upper half of the reptilian Earth Monster. Poets and painters compared her lower half, the hide-bound earth, to a ferocious turtle or a fierce crocodile (see illustration on p.9).

For the most part, descriptions of the gods changed with every story. It was like being at a big party with a thousand people talking at once. Of course, some stories got lost along the way and some got so mixed up it is impossible to know where they started and how far back in time.

Now a few Maya stories were eventually written down in our alphabet. My brief retelling of the Maya creation story, the adventures of the Hero Twins, and the birth of corn are based on the *Popol Vuh*, translated by Dennis Tedlock. Scenes from this great epic first appeared in Maya art more than two thousand years ago. The K'iche

Maya version was translated into Spanish in 1702. The stories are still told, with many variations, throughout the Maya area.

It's true my neighbors talk all day, and some of the tales they tell may be as old as the pyramids. "Lady Yellow Ramon Leaf" and the "Serpent of Fire" were pieced together from scraps told to me by Chol and Lacandon Maya friends Chencho Guzman and Chan Kin Tercero of Palenque. Xun Calixto, a Tzotzil Maya shaman from the mountains of Chiapas, filled in many important details about K'Inich Ahau, god of the sun. Xun says the ancestors, the Fathers-Mothers, taught him the words. Juan Sebastian Canul, like other good storytellers from Yucatan, seems to know Pawahtun intimately. The little god was especially popular among Juan Canul's ancestors, who passed down the stories by word of mouth. Pijul Guzman Mendez says he learned about feathered snakes and bony

THE
STORY *of this* BOOK

centipedes from his grandmother, who heard it from a talking serpent. Pijul says this same boa constrictor created the rainbow.

Other listeners besides me have been fortunate to hear the ancient words retold by living storytellers. The tale of Chak and his serpent daughters first appeared in *Perils of the Soul* by Calixta Guiterrez Holmes. Grandmother Moon is my version of a traditional weaving story told by Loxa Jiménes Lópes and printed in Ambar Past's beautiful book of Maya women's songs and spells, *Incantations*. "The Lazy Buzzard" and "Saved from the Horned Serpent" are based on tales collected and translated by Robert M. Laughlin and published in *Mayan Tales from Zinacantán: Songs and Stories*

from the People of the Bat. My experience editing that book sent me on a lifelong search for more Maya myths and stories. Robert Laughlin told me the story of José de la Fuente Coronado, the boy who discovered Palenque, in hopes that I would write about it one day.

The stories in this book interweave ancient motifs and modern folk tales. Similarly, some of the illustrations are derived from ancient sculptures and painted pots (the Lord of Death, Rabbit, and the Water Lily Jaguar); others are interpretations with a modern Mexican slant. The Maya use the same word, *tsib*, for writing and painting, and it is rare to see one without the other. Together, these stories and illustrations bring the ancient deities to life.

The *Popol Vuh* is often called the Maya Bible, mainly because the Hero Twins' selflessness and sacrifice offer moral lessons to live by. The defeat of death is the theme of all religions. Readers don't have to believe in many creations to understand the cycle of life, death, and rebirth that is at the heart of Maya philosophy. Readers don't have to believe in many gods in order to know we are beholden to the natural forces of sun and rain and to the plants and animals that sustain us.

The stories in this book are my interpretations of Maya art and my versions of other people's versions that are probably centuries old. There is no perfect version. The stories change with each storyteller and grow like all living things in nature.

GLOSSARY
and GUIDE *to*
PRONUNCIATION

SUPERNATURAL BEINGS

Chak (chaak)
Maya rain god

Ehecatl (ay-HAY-catl)
*wind god of central
Mexico, an aspect of
Quetzalcoatl*

Hunahpu
(hoon-ah-POO)
*"One Lord," the first-
born of the Hero Twins*

Ik (eek)
*Maya god of wind
and breath*

Itzamna
(EATS-um-nah)
*Maya creator god,
grandfather of the
Hero Twins*

Kawil (ka-WEEL) *Maya
god of lightning, wind,
fertility, and royal blood*

Kinich Ahau
(kin-ITCH a-haw)
Maya god of the sun

Kolowisi
(ko-low-WIS-ee)
*name for the feathered
or horned serpent
among the Zuni people
of New Mexico*

Kukulcan
(coo-cool-KAHN)
*Maya name for the
Plumed Serpent*

Lamat (la-MAHT)
*Venus, a form of the
Plumed Serpent*

Mixcoatl
(MEESH-ko-atl)
*Cloud Serpent, father
of Tezcatlipoca*

Nagual (nah-GWAL)
animal spirit

Palalukong
(pa-la-loo-KON)
*name for the Plumed
Serpent among the
Hopi people of Arizona*

Pawahtun
(pow-a-tune)
*Maya god who holds up
the sky*

Quetzalcoatl
(ketz-al-KO-atl)
*Aztec name for the
Plumed Serpent, by
which he is best known*

Tzul (tzool)
Rabbit

Xbalanque
(sh-bah-lan-KAY)
"Little Jaguar Sun," the younger brother of the Hero Twins

Xmucane
(SHMOO-kahn-eh)
grandmother of the Hero Twins

Xul Vo' Ton
(shool voh tohn)
the Tzotzil Maya name for the Horned Serpent. His habitat ranges from the Maya area to the Pueblo region of the American Southwest

Tezcatlipoca
(tez-cat-lee-PO-kah)
Aztec name for the "Lord of the Smoking Mirror," god of night and magic and brother of Quetzalcoatl. He shares attributes with the Maya god Kawil.

Topiltzin
(toe-peel-tzeen)
culture hero of the Toltecs, divine king of ancient Tula, in central Mexico

GLOSSARY

Places and People

Calakmul
(kah-lahk-mool)
*Called "Three Stones"
in Classic Maya times,
this powerful Maya
city-state in Campeche,
Yucatan Peninsula, was
ruled by the Lords of
the Snake.*

Chichimec
(chi-chi-meck)
*ancient people of the
northern Mexican
desert*

Chilam Balam
(chi-LAMB bah-LUM)
*"Jaguar Priests," or
seers, who kept books
of history and prophesy*

Copan (Ko-PAN)
*major Maya city-state
and art center in north-
ern Honduras*

K'an Bahlam
(kahn bah-LUM)
*"Serpent Jaguar,"
ruler of Palenque
(A.D. 684–702)*

K'iché (key-CHAY)
*a large Maya group
living in central
Guatemala*

Mixtecs (MEESH-teks)
*"Cloud People," found-
ers of the great Mixtec
civilization of Oaxaca,
Mexico*

Oaxaca (wah-HA-kah)
*modern state in
southwestern Mexico*

Palenque
(pah-LEN-kay)
*known as Lakanja,
Great Waters, during
the Classic period,
this Maya city-state
in Chiapas, Mexico,
was famed for art and
astronomy.*

Tamoanchan
(tam-oh-an-chan)
*mythical land of rain
and mist, perhaps
located near the Gulf of
Mexico*

Teotihuacan
(tay-oh-tee-wah-KAHN)
The "birthplace of the gods," this immense imperial state in the Valley of Mexico had a strong influence on cultures from the American Southwest to Honduras before its collapse in A.D. 650

Tikal (tee-call)
prominent Maya kingdom in the northern rainforest of Guatemala from 400 B.C. to A.D. 900

Toltecs (TOLL-teks)
"artists" and warriors of central Mexico

Tula (TOO-la)
"Place of Reeds," the great city of the Toltecs, in central Mexico

Yaxchilan
(yash-chi-LAN)
Known as "Cleft Sky," this prosperous Maya center controlled trade along the Usumacinta (usu-ma-SIN-ta) River.

Xibalba
(shee-BAHL-bah)
"Place of Fear," the Maya Underworld

Xok (shoke)
Lady "Shark," a powerful Maya queen who ruled Yaxchilan with her husband Shield Jaguar (A.D. 681–742)

GLOSSARY

Plants and Creatures

Ceiba (say-bah) *cottonwood or silk-cotton tree; the Maya Tree of Life whose roots are in the Underworld and whose branches support the heavens*

Chachalacas (cha-cha-LA-kas) *noisy brown birds, resembling chickens, commonly found in southern Texas, Mexico, Central and South America*

Coati (kwa-tee) *a furry, long-snouted animal related to raccoons that inhabits deserts and rainforests from the Southwestern United States to Argentina*

Ocotillo (oh-ko-TEE-yo) *This tall wavy plant, native to the Southwestern United States and northern Mexico, has numerous spiny branches that sprout small*

green leaves and bright red flowers during the rainy season.

Quetzal (keh-TZAL) *rare bird with long blue and green tail feathers, sacred to the Maya*

Ramon (ra-MOAN) *giant tropical tree found in the Maya rainforests, the Caribbean, and the Amazon, produces orange fruits and nutritious nuts (breadnut) that have long served as a food source in times of drought and famine.*

Additional Illustrations

(PAGE viii)
Turquoise Mosaic, Chichen Itza,
drawing by Linda Schele
©David Schele. Courtesy of the
Los Angeles County Museum of Art.

(PAGES v, 3, 100, 101, 104, 105, 106, 107)
Paddler Gods, Tikal
drawing by Linda Schele
©David Schele. Courtesy of the
Los Angeles County Museum of Art.

(PAGE 31)
Number 4
by Alonso Mendez

(PAGES v, 103)
Royal Rabbit Vase
by Alonso Mendez

All Maya borders and decorative motifs
by Pedro Meza
From *Batz'I Luch: Traditional Weaving Designs
of Chiapas*. Walter F. Morris, Jr. and
Pedro Meza Girón. San Cristóbal:
Chiapas Grupos Artesanales de Chiapas, 1975.

INDEX

INDEX